BRIDG

BY

ANNETTE

GRACE

JOHNSON

©

2000

BRIDGET

Copyright © 2000 by Annette G. Johnson

All rights reserved

Copyright Office number: TXu755-596

Copyright date: Sept. 29, 2000

First Printing: 2017

ISBN: 978-0-692-92695-6

To all those who helped me to get to the finish line. My husband, Roger, my writer friend, Rita, my computer friend, Celia, and my family. THANK YOU TO ALL!

But most of all to Our Lord God, without Whom none of this would have been possible.

"Cushlamachree"

(Joy of my heart!)

BRIDGET   Johnson

BRIDGET

CHAPTER I

Still she stood, bare feet rooted to the dirt floor of the cabin, her heart frozen within her. The sound had been almost imperceptible. A slight tremor had tickled the soles of her feet. She heard the gentle clink of cup nudging cup on the open shelf. Then Mary Catherine sat in a chair near the hearth, hardly daring to draw breath, and drew on her stringless brogans.

Hurrying footsteps padded down the path past her house

BRIDGET	Johnson

and drew her to the door. Her hand reached out to the latch. To go out would be to know. She could not stay her hand, for she must know what had become of Michael.

She followed the crowd up the mile-long path to the brow of the hill. The women with a smattering of men quieted in expectation, gathering around the entrance to the coal mine. Here each day loads of hard coal, black diamonds of eons past, rolled out in miniature rail cars.

Dumped and picked over by young boys sitting at the top of the breaker, the castaway waste ringed the patch with culm hills.

Mary Catherine made her way through the crowd, drawing near the shaft just behind a knot of men.

Mr. Williams, the mine superintendent, stepped forward in the haze of spring twilight and faced the throng.

"There's been an accident."

The gruff announcement, bereft of emotion, sent a shock of

BRIDGET

dread through the crowd that hemmed her in. Then came a groan.

"Who?" a quavering female voice asked.

"We don't know yet. Go back to your homes."

No one moved to go, and a shudder passed through Mary Catherine again from those amassed about her. Mr. Williams turned and strode to the breaker building, now empty of the boys who separated coal from slag, and spoke a few words to the foreman who stood waiting there.

Then Langdon, the foreman, stepped forward.

"It's only the second year of this bloody war, and the Union will need all the coal they can get. So you women best go home now."

A whirlpool of voices lapped outward to the edge of the crowd, and Mary Catherine heard the muted violence in the words as they surged over her.

"Men dead, you can bet."

BRIDGET   Johnson

"Why don't they just say it?"

"They probably don't even know what happened."

"Where's my Billy?"

"He'll be all right. You'll see."

"If they was all right, they'd be glad to say it. You can bet someone's dead."

Michael, oh Michael, where are you? Her mind reached out to him, willing him to live.

Michael, do you remember when we met? Me just turned eighteen and you a grown man of twenty-one.

As pitch-dark night descended on the hills of Pennsylvania, lighted only by staggering torches in the hands of the miners, Mary Catherine's thoughts took wing back across the ocean to that beloved land.

BRIDGET

BRIDGET

CHAPTER II

The year that the blight first visited Eire Mary Catherine had just turned sixteen. That spring birds trilled their songs and grass waved emerald on the hillsides just outside Cork. The air so soft it wrapped a person round in its down warm folds. A girl so glad to be alive she ran to those southern hills, hair flying, till she could run no more. Then she twirled and twirled, flinging herself onto the grass, and watched the azure sky and clouds spin round

BRIDGET   Johnson

and round in dizzying array.

She stared up at the passing clouds, wiggling her toes at the sun. His face, shaped by each great white fluff that spun by, recalled her first sight of him at the town fair. Dark he was of eye and hair. And he had glanced at her, too. His look had caused a sudden hot flood to course through her, which had sent her running to these hills, so dear to her.

This strange sensation confused her. How could the look of one young man among many set her so ill at ease? She put her hand over her heart and felt it racing.
How could one moment so change a girl?

After calming herself, she rose and retraced her steps, pondering these things.

"Where have you been, my girl?" her father asked.

Standing by his cart in the Cork town square, brows

BRIDGET   Johnson

storming over his blue eyes, he feigned sternness. The eyes, her own clear blue, twinkled and belied his tight lips. Ringlets of smoke curled above his head, and the sweet aroma from his pipe drifted to her.

"Why, Da, I had a bit of a run, that's all."

"We've sold what little we brought to market. So we'll be on our way now."

Giving her a hug round the shoulders, he pushed her gently forward.

"Go help your mother now. Find your brothers and we'll be goin'."

The family followed the empty cart her father guided as the pony pulled it along the road toward home. Nearing the stone-walled, sod-roofed house Mary Catherine ran ahead.

She wondered what it would be like to leave this house. For someday she would marry and leave Mother and Father and

BRIDGET   Johnson

cleave to her husband as the parish priest had

read from scripture.

    Resting where road met path, only a few steps from their door, she considered this place, having known no other. The stones of various shapes and sizes reposed one on another in a friendly almost loving fashion, some gray as a day blessed by rain, others the color of a dulled sun. She knew every crack and crevice of them and touched them now as she walked close. The rough hewn door welcomed her there, giving way to her tender press upon its oaken board.

    Hearing her parents approach, she caught enough of what they said to send the

slightest alarm through her.

    "The potatoes will run out before midsummer, Sean. Then what'll we do?"

    "Hush, woman, the children'll hear. The next crop looks

BRIDGET   Johnson

good. We'll be careful and eat a little less till it comes."

Mary Catherine turned just inside the small house and stood in the shadow of the hearth, holding her breath, listening, and twisting a lock of her raven hair. Then peeking round the corner, she searched her father's face for the truth. His skin pulled taut about his mouth betrayed the only sign of his concern. Her mother's brow had assumed its natural pose of loving care. Nothing here for her to worry herself about.

With the coming of summer the leaves started to brown on the potato plants. And the crop looked to be prime, according to her father. She along with her brothers worked each spade-full of earth her father turned. Sifting the soil with her hands, Mary Catherine pulled the small, earth encrusted orbs from the bottom of the plant, and tossed them into the wooden bucket to be cleaned later.

"Mary Catherine, we'll be havin' a few of the new crop for

BRIDGET Johnson

supper," her mother called to her from the house.

Stooped over the bucket she had set on the bench outside the door, Mary Catherine detected a foul musty odor she hadn't noticed when plucking them one by one. She took water from another bucket sitting there and splashed it over the earth-stained mess. Then grasping one misshapen sphere, the putrid lump in her hand resembled nothing edible. She reached down again, now on her knees, the corruption so close she feared it would sicken her.

Looking skyward she expected to see it darkening, for sure she was that a shadow passed over the land in that moment.

Panic gnawed at her stomach.

"Mother, they're spoiled. Look," she said, stretching her arm toward the doorway of the house, her fingers slimed with the blackened pulp.

Her mother came to her side and glanced at her, then at her

hand, dread etched on her brow.

"I'll get your father. He'll know what to do."

While her mother rushed from the house to the fields, Mary Catherine scraped the stinking mess from her hands.

That evening around the table they sat silent, the terror of hunger imprisoning

their tongues.

"We'll have to eat what we can of the new crop before they've all spoiled," her father near whispered. "After that I'll find something for us, even if we have to eat the rent."

He stared at his plate as he spoke, his voice edged with a new note she could not discern. It chilled her to hear it.

"But, Da, what is it?" Mary Catherine asked.

"I'm not sure. A sickness, I've heard, has come across the sea. We'll save the mite we have left from the old crop."

"Little indeed it is," said her mother.

BRIDGET   Johnson

"Will there be enough for the winter?" her brother Patrick asked, the oldest of her three younger brothers.

Thinking of his own stomach, Mary Catherine supposed, and sent a scowl his way.

"I hope so," said her father. "But make a special request in your evenin' prayers, my lad."

Mary Catherine watched her father, intent upon his every word. Now he raised his head, and clenching a cold, empty pipe in his teeth and their eyes met. She knew he would expect much of her in the days to come.

"Mary Catherine, would you lead the prayer, before we eat what the Lord has provided?"

"Bless us, O Lord," she prayed.

BRIDGET

BRIDGET

CHAPTER III

"Mother, I should go."

"There's no need."

"I'm seventeen now. I should be helpin' the family."

"One crop does not spell failure. Wait."

Wait Mary Catherine did, through winter and spring. The potato plants sprouted up green and tender. Hope traveled the land on that spring's zephyr.

BRIDGET   Johnson

But within the month the wilt appeared, crushing expectations. Black '47. A spirit of despair descended and oppressed the land.

"Mother, may I go now? I can earn a few pence to relieve the burden of the house."

"Where?" Mary Catherine, where would you go?"

"I heard in Cork, they're lookin' for help in Liverpool. Our People are sick and
dyin' there."

"They're dyin' here, too."

"I know. But there I can earn a little to help us."

The sadness in her mother's face, when she looked on it, held a hopelessness Mary Catherine had not seen there before.

"Besides, most of the sick there are our own," Mary Catherine said. "On their way to America, for they couldn't pay the rent."

BRIDGET

Her mother seemed to pay no heed to her.

"Couldn't Da put off payin' the rent?"

"He's done that."

Flat and weary, her mother's tone almost unnerved her.

"We've held back on givin' the landlord the oats and the hens. Now they're gone and we've nothin' left."

"Has he spoken to the landlord?"

"He has."

"Well, what did the landlord say?"

"He said we must meet the quota to be shipped. If that happens then he'd have to put us off the land."

Mary Catherine went to her mother and knelt by her chair.

"You see, don't you, Mother?" putting her head on her mother's lap, "I must go.
One less mouth to feed."

"I don't doubt you'll do well. But we'll miss you smilin'

BRIDGET

face. You've been such a help to me and your father. But, you're right. Our people need your gentle touch. I'm sure there aren't many who would help the starvin' wretches."

Mary Catherine rose, and standing behind her mother's chair, encircled her mother's shoulders with her arms, then laid her head alongside her neck.

Within the week she wheedled passage on a fishing boat bound from Cork to Dublin, and with the few pence her mother pressed into her hand at her leaving she ferried across the Irish Sea to Liverpool. A friend of her mother's in Cork had given her the name of the doctor in charge of the hospital near the port.

Drawn faces of hunger lined her way along the wharf. And the rags that passed for clothing hung on their shrunken frames. Many an ashen, pleading countenance turned to her as she inquired of the hospital's whereabouts.

She picked her way down one dark alley after another

BRIDGET   Johnson

cluttered with broken boxes and human waste, causing her to pinch her nostrils against the stench. Coming upon a windowless warehouse, a structure beaten down and weathered gray by salt air, she stared in disbelief. This cannot be.

Lifting the latch, she pushed hard upon the cracked dry wood of the door. The heavy portal creaked open but stopped as she eased the pressure. She thrust herself against the door with renewed effort, and a cloud of fetid foul air rushed over her, revealing a cavernous void of dust and shadows within. In the dim interior she detected movement as her eyes adjusted to the gloom, while struggling to keep from retching.

A dusky figure stepped toward her out of the shadows, evoking a momentary fright.

"My name is Dr. Robertson," he said, waving her forward in an imperial manner. "And who might you be?"

His tall, gaunt frame looked more like the spirit of death

BRIDGET   Johnson

than that of a doctor. He lacked but a scythe.

"I've come to help. I'm Mary Catherine Coyne."

"We need all the hands anyone can spare," said Dr. Robertson.

Leading the way down a narrow path of floor, the he pointed left, then right, indicating what appeared to be bundles of rags laying on dirty straw.

"Have you any experience nursing the sick?"

She would have answered, but something caught at her skirt. Glancing down, she pulled at her garment, trying to free it. The creature she found attached to it clawed at her again, mouthing gibberish she couldn't understand. Mary Catherine wrenched her dress away and bent over to better observe her attacker.

Once freed of the support of the garment the woman had slumped over backwards, gasping. Mary Catherine touched the woman's forehead and found it to be on fire with fever.

BRIDGET   Johnson

"I would ask you again if you have any experience, but I see you at least have good instincts."

"I've helped my mother care for my brothers. Some, too, with our neighbors. And once in awhile aided the village doctor."

I suppose that'll have to do. You'll be assigned to one of the women with more practice, at first. Then we'll see."

With that he strode off down the row of sick and disappeared in the shadows.

Abandoned, Mary Catherine warily glanced about, trying by the light of dim lanterns hung on a few bearing posts to discriminate the human forms from the heaps of straw and refuse. At times the groans and wailing rose to a crescendo, echoing off the windowless walls, then quieted to puling and whimpering.

During the following months she washed fever ravished bodies, fed a thin broth to those with the pox, and comforted with crooning words those dying of the dreaded sickness, dark purple buboes prominent in their armpits and groins.

These sick, refugees of her own Erin, lay captive in Liverpool, felled by their illness and starving. A grim reminder of the horror she had seen outside her family's door and along the roads on her journey. Men and women with haunted looks. And the children so old looking. Young faces so wizened by hunger that they had appeared to be diminutive likenesses of their own grandparents.

Along those same roads as she had trod her way to Cork, wagons had passed her laden with barrels of grain, other fresh produce, and pigs or chickens boxed and bound for Cork City port to be shipped to England. She had asked herself how that could be with her own people starving? How could the landlords have sent the food away?

She had remembered then something her father had said with a flash of anger in his voice.

BRIDGET   Johnson

"We grow grain and raise animals as rent to his lordship. The potatoes what is left is all we have to keep death from our door. If the potato dies, we'll have to eat the rent. Then there'll be nothin' left."

Wiping the sweat from the fevered brows under her hand, Mary Catherine understood. Some of these diseased souls might yet live. Those dying of starvation in a land of plenty would not. Dying of the sickness might be quicker.

She learned much of death. Some went peacefully, not crying out.

"Thank you, darlin' girl. Your mother and father must be proud."

Others, crazed with pain and burning, she spent herself cooing into calmness.

"You're killin' me!" one shouted.

"I know you, you want me dead," accused another.

BRIDGET — Johnson

"You're poisonin' me."

This one knocked the soup from her hand, the wooden bowl clattering across the floor.

So much sickness and death changed everyone, even her, she knew. Before she had come she had been a giddy girl, a child. Working with these pitiable mortals had altered her forever. A woman grown she had become.

BRIDGET

CHAPTER IV

The vision of the shrunken forms left her as Mary Catherine felt a stroke upon her arm. Esther, her buxom blonde self, stood by her side.

"Mary Catherine. We should go home. There'll be no news this night."

"I know."

"Then come away. We'll know soon enough when the dead

wagon comes."

Putting her arm about Mary Catherine's waist, Esther guided her down the hill through the crowd. As they emerged from the throng a hand slipped into Mary Catherine's on her other side. She knew without looking that the tender touch came from Anne Marie, a countrywoman from Erin. A painful smile twisted Mary Catherine's lips. She squeezed the hands of her friends as the three plodded with heavy steps down the dark path.

"The children," said Mary Catherine in a stunned voice, bringing her friends to a sudden halt. "I left them still at supper."

Dropping her friends' hands, she ran toward her gate.

"When your children are asleep, Mary Catherine," Anne Marie called after her, "come to my house."

Opening the cabin door, Mary Catherine beheld her eldest daughter, Catherine Marie, sitting before the hearth fire, holding a finger to her lips. She glanced toward Sean's cot and heard the

BRIDGET

purr of his snore.

"I put the younger ones to bed, Mama," said her daughter.

"It's good you are to your old mother, Catherine Marie."

"Is everything all right at the mines?"

"No one knows yet, Catherine."

Then sitting down near her daughter, she put her arm around the girl's shoulder.

"You best go to bed now. We'll know more by morning, I'd not be surprised."

Later that night Mary Catherine and Esther sat around the table in Anne Marie's cabin as she set the kettle for tea to boiling over the hearth fire.

"Jack will come with news as soon as he hears," said Anne Marie.

"He wasn't caught, then," said Mary Catherine.

"No. The explosion happened in a tunnel far down the

BRIDGET   Johnson

line."

"Then some of the men got out?" said Esther.

"Only a few, so far," Anne Marie said. "But I'm sure most will be found safe."

"My Emil has lived through accidents before," said Esther. "I expect he'll survive this one."

"So has Michael. He worked other mines before we came to Locust Gap."

"One time Emil and the boys were eating lunch, and the rats instead of coming for their share were running for the exit. You never seen men leave a meal so fast in your life, said my Emil. He should talk. He made it out before the boys."

"Thank God for the rats," said Anne Marie. "And I never thought I'd be sayin' that."

"I recall a cave-in in a patch in the Southern Field, where we lived when we first came to Pennsylvania maybe ten years ago now," said Mary Catherine. "Michael had worked in one of the upper shafts that spring day. There had been a lot of rain the week before. Well, the men in the lower shafts weren't so lucky. The mine was flooded and many men were drowned or crushed by rotted timbers."

The three women paused, lost in the throes of past anguish.

A breath escaped Anne Marie's lips, hardly noticeable as a sigh.

"Jack worked on the docks in New York, and I worked as a maid before we came here," she said. "Jack said there was no future there, so here we are now."

"My Emil's brothers got the farm in Germany," said Esther, "so, we decided to try our luck here. Just like us to come with a war in the offing." "My boys just had to join up. I only had the two, and I don't know what piece of ground they're fighting over now."

BRIDGET   Johnson

"I had a baby once," said Anne Marie, taking the kettle from the hearth. "She'd be about Fiona's age now, if she had lived."

Mary Catherine glanced at Esther, but Esther shook her head. No need to ask.

Anne Marie brewed then poured the tea. Mary Catherine, lifting her cup, waited for Anne Marie to resume her tale, if and when she wished.

"The family I worked for were kind," Anne Marie said, failing to say anything of the baby. " But we were servants, don't you know. It's like they really didn't see us. She called me Bridget."

"But that's not your name," said Esther, indignation resonating in her words.

Mary Catherine said nothing, for she knew the answer. She'd heard it before from other young Irish women.

BRIDGET Johnson

"She called all of us Bridget. That is everyone that was Catholic and Irish."

"Well, of all the shiftless things I've ever heard of," Esther said, huffing her dissatisfaction with the gentry.

"It was back in '54 that we came. Things had gotten better by then. But Jack was determined to come. He'd been listenin' to his brother about America and how much better off we'd be if we'd come. As luck would have it we came by way of Dublin to Canada. Our landlord arranged passage on one of those coffin ships. It was free, you see. They were that glad to be rid of us Irish."

"Was Jack's brother in Canada?" asked Esther.

"No. He'd shipped straight to Boston."

Anne Marie took a long draught of tea.

"I didn't tell Jack. But I was carryin' our child by the time we boarded ship."

BRIDGET

"Did you lose it at sea?" asked Mary Catherine.

"No, at Grosse Isle. Our ship was nothin' like the coffin ships of the past, I hear. The landlords cared not a whit if they were even seaworthy back then. But conditions were bad enough. The foul water, the starvin' food limitin' on board. Then the sickness. First seasickness, then the ship's fever."

"We had a few died of the fever when we crossed, too," said Esther.

"I got the fever just as we made port. So they put me in a hospital there, if you'd call it that. Nothin' but a tent and so cold. The baby came then. She'd caught the fever from me and came dead. I longed to die, for I'd killed my baby."

A shudder shook Anne Marie as she finished.

Esther reached across the table and swallowed Anne Marie's hand with her own ample one.

"Anne Marie, you couldn't be to blame," said Mary

BRIDGET Johnson

Catherine. "It was the fever did it, not you."

"I know that now. What I was witness to on that island you wouldn't believe. By the time I recovered, Jack had already made a little coffin for our baby and buried her."

A moment of silence passed as the women grieved the lost children.

"Jack took me to her grave before we left. The buryin' ground looked strange. Heaps of earth. Small hills that didn't match the rest of the island. Jack confessed that the mounds were mass graves. Many bodies thrown in a hole. Some not given a coffin, some not even a shroud."

Mary Catherine took hold of Anne Marie's other hand as her friend lifted her eyes to her. Tears spilled down Anne Marie's cheeks at the touch.

"Jack showed me where he'd found a bit of unspoiled ground. He'd put her in the earth there. Scrounging the island for just the proper rock, he'd scraped her name on it and the year of her birth."

"What name did he give her?" asked Mary Catherine.

"Mary. He gave her to the Blessed Mother's keepin'."

"Good," said Mary Catherine.

Yes, good. Better than the babe she had left buried in the wood.

BRIDGET   Johnson

BRIDGET

CHAPTER V

Mary Catherine's few shillings had staved off hunger for her family the winter of black '47. But her father grew ill and her mother called her home. Her father seeming on the mend the following spring, the family made plans to attend the fair in Cork.

Making inquiries, Mary Catherine found that the name of the young man from Cork that she had often dreamt about was Michael McNurney. Come fair day she danced down the road in

BRIDGET   Johnson

anticipation, pirouetting on her bare toes. In spare moments of ladylike decorum she entertained doubts, which in turn led to confusion. To gather her thoughts she glanced back to her parents and brothers who trudged behind. Her father brought no cart laden with things to sell this fair day.

Her mother and father smiled at her. Twinges of guilt pricked her amid her joy at the impending glimpse she might have of Michael. A new beginning could be made to a new season, she hoped. After all, the blight hadn't appeared as yet. It might be over.

With renewed excitement she twirled, whirling out her ankle-length skirt. The same blue as her eyes, her father had said.

Coming abreast of the Kennedy family, also cartless this year, Mary Catherine grew quiet and sedate before their two little girls. Her skipping and running days were numbered, she knew, and it wouldn't do to give bad example to the little ones.

BRIDGET Johnson

    This fair day as in the past all appeared gay and festive in spite of few hens and fewer vegetables, and only a trifling few pies to be bought and fewer pence to buy them with. Still Mary Catherine sensed a desperate gaiety amongst the fairgoers. The crowd gathered in the square, the women bedecked in frocks of yellow, blue, and green, a bit worn but still bright, ribbons tied gaily in their hair. The men argued friendly-like over the merits of their horses. Races were run.

    Mary Catherine searched her neighbors' faces, aware that some friends did not appear amidst the throng. Even if a mist of sadness sometimes mingled with the joy, on the whole she felt it to be a good day. Studying the ground beneath her feet, she furtively glanced about searching for his face. The back of his head came into view first. His black curls as dark as her own long tresses moved to the gentle breeze. Seen over a bay pony's back that shock of curls she'd have known anywhere, untamed as it was.

BRIDGET

He turned and she looked away. For she knew they couldn't be caught staring at each other in public. Spying her mother, Mary Catherine hurried to her side.

"Mother, where are the boys?"

Her mother smiled.

"They're well enough. You needn't worry. They're lookin' at that pony, just there."

Her mother nodded in the direction of the pony that moments earlier had drawn her own attention.

"If you wish to know how they are, why not ask them?"

Suspicious, Mary Catherine scrutinized her mother's face for the mischief that she had heard in her tone. She detected no artifice in the older woman's countenance. Turning once again to the pony, she strolled with deliberate tread, head high, intent on seeking out her brothers.

"Jimmy, Patrick – are you bein' careful of Sean?"

BRIDGET   Johnson

Four faces regarded her as she felt a warmth spread up her neck to her cheeks. She raised her hand to the side of her face, hoping to hide the flush she felt to be there. Too late. The smile on Michael's lips proved he had already taken notice.

"Go along with you, boys," said Mary Catherine. "Mother's been huntin' for you."

Turning on her heel, she didn't look back to see if they followed.

"Mary Catherine's got a beau," Patrick chanted as he ran after her. "Mary Catherine's got a fella."

"Hush, boy, or I'll box your ears for you," Mary Catherine said.

"You and who else?"

"Hush, I say."

Approaching her mother who sat near the booth that held the baked goods, Mary

Catherine watched as her mother's brow puckered in puzzlement.

"Mother, I found them for you."

"Found them for me?"

"Mary Catherine's got a fella," mimicked Jimmy.

Mary Catherine glared at her brother, wishing him swallowed up by the earth under him. Feeling her mother's wondering look upon her, she decided to brave it out. She settled on the bench beside her mother and pretended indifference to the teasing.

"Patrick, you and Jimmy take Sean to see the pigs," said their mother.

"Pigs?" said Patrick and Jimmy in chorus.

"What do we want to see pigs for?" asked Jimmy.

Only Sean showed any signs of moving.

"Be off with the bunch of you. I wish to speak to your sister without you gawkin' about."

Her brothers turned and fled.

"Now my girl, what is this?"

"Nothin', Mother. I don't even know the man."

"What man?"

She knew she'd put her foot in it now.

"I haven't spoken to him. I don't even know if he'd want to meet the likes of me."

"And why not, I ask. Why wouldn't any man want to meet the fairest girl in Cork? Is he blind?"

Abashed, Mary Catherine plowed a little furrow in the earth with her toe.

"Well, enjoy the fair, my girl. I'll speak to your father about this later."

Mary Catherine escaped further discussion and just as devoutly avoided being within the sight of Michael McNurney.

BRIDGET

CHAPTER VI

After kneeling beside her bed to say her prayers that night, Mary Catherine lay awake listening and caught a few words as they passed between her mother and father.

"There'll have to be a meetin'," said her father.

"For certain," said her mother.

"I'll speak to himself."

"Soon," her mother said.

BRIDGET   Johnson

"Soon," Mary Catherine whispered to herself in the dark.

Except for the odd stolen glimpse of Michael on the road to Cork City, Mary Catherine exchanged only the briefest of proper greetings with him in the market square. For until they were betrothed she understood that according to custom both Michael and she would be accompanied by one or both parents to assure their behavior was decent.

And just so, during the waning summer, visits were made by Mary Catherine and her parents to the McNurney house, followed by reciprocal calls upon the Coyne household by Michael and his parents. Their fathers discussed the settling of her dowry and the land that would come to Michael.

On a blustery fall evening that smelled of damp, decaying foliage the families gathered, and the rotund Mr. McNurney heartily commanded, "Raise your glasses."

The warm hearth fire of the McNurney house brightened

the mood within as Michael smiled at her from across the table. The toe of his shoe touched hers, sending a thrill through her. Lifting her eyes to his, he knew she was lost forever. Oh, Michael, her heart beat out.

"I give you the young couple," said Mr. McNurney, "betrothed this day."

"Aye," said her father.

Glancing toward her mother, Mary Catherine discovered her chatting animatedly with Mrs. McNurney. No doubt the two were busily planning her trousseau and wedding.

Mary Catherine winked at Michael.

"We're in for it now," Michael whispered, grinning at her.

"Well, Mary Catherine," said Mr. McNurney, "what do you think of my boy?"

Startled at being addressed by her future father-in-law, Mary Catherine raised her eyes to his as her cheeks burned.

BRIDGET   Johnson

"I like him well enough, I reckon," she said.

With that everyone in the room roared with laughter. She couldn't think for the life of her what she'd said that had been so entertaining.

One bleak night in mid-autumn the sheriff's men came to the Coyne house, sent by the landlord, and dragged her father from it, beat him, then threw him into the ditch that ran alongside the road. She and her mother were unceremoniously plucked from the cottage and dumped upon the roadside. Her younger brothers, who kicked and struck at their tormentors, were tossed into the ditch like so much rubbish.

When the sheriff's men torched the house, what little dowry she had managed to
scrape together burned, sending firefly ashes into the night. In desolation Mary Catherine and her family camped beside the road within sight of the ruins that had been their home.

BRIDGET

Mary Catherine then learned what her father had kept secret from them. Since the potatoes had blackened again that year, they had eaten the rent. Foraging through the ruins, Mary Catherine, Patrick, and Jimmy sought anything with which to cover themselves. The family huddled together, and in their misery the rain began. By morning little Sean had developed a hacking cough.

Sitting on a rock by the side of the road, Mary Catherine held her head in her hands in the gray dawn.

"I've no dowry," she bemoaned. "Who'd want me now?"

"I would."

Parting her fingers, she peeked through them to see Michael standing just a few feet away on the road. He strode toward her and took hold of her wrists, the strength of him bringing a momentary twinge of pain, then pulled her to her feet.

"We'll marry now, Mary Catherine. We'll not wait. What's

BRIDGET   Johnson

the use of waitin'?"

"Now?"

The word stuck halfway up her throat. She couldn't be sure it had come out. So she repeated it.

"Now?"

Saying it again seemed to make it all more real and not a vision as she had suspected at first. For who had ever heard of such a thing as being picked up off the road and wed?

"Today. It's all arranged."

She shook with the chill and Michael took her hands in his.

"Your hands are cold. I'll warm them," he said and rubbed them between his palms.

Putting his arm around her waist, he drew her close, and the warmth of him stilled her shivering. Together they gathered up her family and slogged along the rutted road, slipping and sliding in

BRIDGET								Johnson

the muck.

Michael's sprightly mother ushered them all in with a cordial smile, and she soon had them sitting around the hearth fire, shrugging and flapping off their dampness like so many setting, fretting hens. She then brought them some thin tea that tasted like the finest nectar to Mary Catherine, after that night's rude treatment.

Once the Coyne family were warmed, the two mothers conferred then led Mary Catherine into Mr. and Mrs. McNurney's bedroom. There they gave her a clean shift to wear. Mary Catherine had donned her blue dress before being thrown out on the roadside, and now she watched as her mother brushed it near the fireplace, grooming the damp and grime out of it.

Bringing the garment to her, her mother helped her dress as Mrs. McNurney arranged the wedding dinner. Her mother then placed a circlet of holly berries wound round with a bit of white

BRIDGET   Johnson

lace on Mary Catherine's hair.

"There, my girl, I've done all a mother can do. Good luck and God bless ye."

Her mother opened the bedroom door, kissed her on the cheek, and pressed her forward. Mary Catherine stepped out into the main room now aglow with candles and firelight. The room appeared overcrowded with the two families, made even more so when a rap on the door brought the parish priest in to join them round the table. The black-cassocked cleric took his place at the head of the table, the place of honor, with Mary Catherine to one side of him and Michael on the other. Her family took their places near her, and Michael's family gathered on his side. And so they were wed.

After the ceremony Michael's mother, assisted by her own mother, set the meal upon the board. Roast piglet, one of only two left on the place, graced the center of the table, golden and smelling like heaven to Mary Catherine. A trencher piled high with cornmeal cakes was passed. Michael's father poured both wine and whiskey, carefully hoarded, for the toasts. Then they set the table to the side, where the youngsters perched, watching as their elders prepared to dance. Thereupon Mr. McNurney brought out a fiddle and sawed a reel and more, before lapsing into the sweet, old tunes.

After the priest left, the two mothers once more led Mary Catherine into the bedroom.

"I wish you to have this for I have no daughters of me own to pass it on to," said Mrs. McNurney, placing in Mary Catherine's hands a pink cotton sleeping gown. "It's from me own wedding night."

"I couldn't...."

"You're the wife of my first born. You must take it."

Mary Catherine threw her arms about her mother-in-law's

neck and kissed her on the cheek.

"You'll have your first night together in this bed where Michael was born."

Wiping her eyes, Mrs. McNurney quit the room, leaving Mary Catherine with her own mother.

"Mary Catherine, you're a woman grown."

Looking at her mother, Mary Catherine glimpsed a tear trembling on the tip of her mother's lower lash.

"You've grown so quick."

She watched the droplet steal down her mother's cheek.

"Darlin' girl, be happy."

Her mother gave her a brief hug and slipped out the door.

Once left alone Mary Catherine changed into the soft gown and crept beneath the coverlet. A moment later the door opened, and in the lighted space stood Michael. Closing the door behind him, he blew out the flame in the lone candle that stood upon the shelf near the door. Darkness covered them.

    She heard his clothing drop upon the floor. Then the bed moved with his weight.

    "Come close," Michael murmured as his arm drew her body to him.

    "My wife," Michael whispered in her ear.

    "My husband," Mary Catherine whispered back.

BRIDGET

CHAPTER VII

The delights of the wedding were overtaken and bedimmed during the seasons that followed. Michael's father had given his son a rood of his own acre to till and plant, and the two families raised a small one-room house for the wedded couple, gathering stones for the walls from the fields.

In the succeeding spring once again the families hoped the potato would hold. Since the Coynes and McNurneys domiciled together now, the Coyne family helped work the fields for they had need of a good crop. But the potato wilted and failed as before. To lift the burden on the house the Coyne family tramped into Cork City whenever a soup kitchen opened, even though by doing so they knew they would all be marked by their friends and neighbors as "soupers". Mary Catherine could hardly hold her head up in public, but hold it high she did in defiance.

One day Sean, her youngest brother, not yet strong enough to make the journey to Cork, stayed behind. The cough that had begun that first night after they were evicted in the storm had never left him. Sitting by his side, Mary Catherine nursed him as she had nursed so many others at the warehouse before him who had suffered with the fever. She bathed his sweating brow, held his hot hands, and clasped him to her bosom when the coughing racked him. Tears spilled from her eyes as she sensed that nothing she did would stave off the thief of the night. At summer's end one morning Sean was no more. He had died in their mother's arms

BRIDGET   Johnson

during the night.

After the mass for the dead in the church alongside the graveyard, Michael and their fathers lowered Sean's shrouded body into the grave. Her mother's haggard face bore eyes ringed with grief. The lines had deepened round her mouth and all color had left her countenance. Her father averted his eyes from his son's crypt, put his arms around Mary Catherine and her mother, and led them away.

Being the blight had taken the potato again that year, Mary Catherine had concealed that she was with child.

"My girl, you best tell Michael," said her mother.

"Tell him what?"

"You know what I mean," her mother said, having paid an unexpected call on her that day well into the fall. "That you're in the family way."

"I'm afraid to say that a new mouth will need to be fed."

BRIDGET

"It's our hope you bear. A new life, a new future."

"Mother, if 'tis a boy, I wish to name him Sean."

Her mother, silent for a moment, spoke in a low voice.

"Your brother would be pleased."

The ashen days of fall blew away in the bitter wind of winter. The women rationed what little food the families scraped together and turned and mended their clothes to make do. The faces around Mary Catherine grew thinner. She protested when her mother and Michael forced precious bits of food into her hands, for she had confessed her condition. When she urged Michael to share equally in the scraps, he became angered.

"'Tis the babe we are feedin'. You must give in and be strong."

"But, Michael, it pains me to see everyone so lean and me alone grow more rounded."

"The next crop will be better. All we need do is hold on till then."

During those cold months they made their bed near the hearth so as not to waste the warmth. Using small pieces of well-worn shifts and castoffs, Mary Catherine sat before the glowing coals and fashioned the wee garments and blankets that would be needed for the babe.

A few days before Christmas she awoke feeling uncomfortable, for her belly had swollen and tightened. She slipped gently from her bed so as not to waken Michael. Wrapping a shawl about herself, Mary Catherine walked in the predawn light to the house of their parents. She rapped gently on the door and waited, shivering, for someone to come. Her own mother opened the door to her, and Mary Catherine fell into her mother's arms.

"What's wrong, Mary Catherine?"

Looking up at her mother, a face so drawn the cheekbones

seemed to push through the skin, she said, "I don't know, Mother. I wish to speak with you."

"What's the whisperin' about?" said Mrs. McNurney, stifling a yawn with the back of her hand, while shuffling toward them.

"I don't know yet. It's Mary Catherine has come."

"Well, have her sit by the fire. I'll brew a little tea."

Without another word Mrs. McNurney set a kettle to heat over the hearth fire, poking the embers to life. Mary Catherine's mother drew a chair to the hearth for her only daughter.

"Now, my girl, what brings you out so early?" said Mrs. McNurney, settling herself on a small bench opposite them before the fire.

They spoke in hushed tones so as not to rouse the rest of the house.

"I felt a bit strange this mornin'. My belly is awful tight."

BRIDGET   Johnson

"How long has this been goin' on?" asked her mother.

"Only for a little while."

Mary Catherine marked the glance that passed between the mothers.

"The baby's comin'?" she asked.

They turned to her and nodded in accord. She didn't know whether to be afraid or excited. Holding herself still, Mary Catherine waited for something to tell her what to feel.

Just then a fierce cramping wrenched her breath away.

"Oh," she gasped.

"It's started," yelped Mrs. McNurney, jumping up.

"Everyone up!" she called out to the room, then rousted her husband from his bed.

"Woman, what are you about?" said Mr. McNurney grumpily.

BRIDGET   Johnson

"We've need of the room. We're havin' a baby in this house. Go and tell your son."

Supporting Mary Catherine on both sides, the mothers led her into the bedroom just as Mr. McNurney, one leg in his trousers, limped out.

"Everything off but your shift and into bed with you," said Mrs. McNurney.

"Here I'll help you," her mother said.

Together they readied Mary Catherine for her child bed.

Soon the clanging of pots and Mrs. McNurney's scolding from the outer room apprised Mary Catherine that the house was being readied for the birthing. Then the pain came and she grabbed onto her mother's hand. Shuddering through her, the spasms stretched her on the rack for a time. How long she couldn't guess. The agony ceased and she took a deep breath.

"That's right, Cushlamachree, rest all you can," whispered

BRIDGET   Johnson

her mother. "It'll be some time till it comes."

All the morning the torturous pains came, each stronger than the last, till Mary Catherine thought she could endure it no longer. Sometime at the beginning she had heard Michael's voice in the house. Knowing he was near consoled her. Her body stretched rigid with pain, her back ached, and her legs shook uncontrollably. Then a wave of torment held her in its grip, enveloping her senses. She begged for it to stop. But the torment grew. She screamed and knew no more. She dreamt that she had died. Her brother, Sean, greeted her and kissed her goodbye as he delivered her back to life with a smile. Then her eyes opened to darkness. Is this death? Movement brought pain, and she moaned. With the sound of her own voice she realized that she lived.

"Michael," she called out, her voice but a whisper.

He must have been waiting near the door for with her call the door opened and he rushed to her side.

"Love, are you all right?"

"Oh, Michael, is it over?"

"Yes, Love. You have given me a son. The best of Christmas presents."

"Will it be all right, Michael, if…."

"Yes. We'll name him Sean. Rest now," Michael said as he bent and kissed her brow.

BRIDGET

CHAPTER VIII

The distant rattle of wheels on the flinty road brought Mary Catherine to her feet. She glanced at Esther and Anne Marie, who had also risen from their chairs. Soon they detected the clopping of hooves and the crunch of stones as the burden of iron banded, wooden wheels crushed them.

"It's the dead wagon," said Mary Catherine in a hushed voice.

BRIDGET   Johnson

The complaining axles stopped outside the door.

Esther, reaching the door first, flung it open to reveal the shape of men, mules, and wagon without. Two lanterns splayed golden halos about their carriers' feet, bracketing the wagon front and back.

"It's Emil," Esther cried. "He's all right."

Rushing to the lantern bearer at the front of the wagon, Esther took hold of Emil's arm just as the mules moved forward down the road. Mary Catherine stood watching, tears blurring her vision to half. She felt relief for Esther mixed with a beginning sadness for herself.

"Come back," said Anne Marie as she took hold of Mary Catherine's arm, and pulled her inside the shanty, closing the door.

"I'll make us another cup of tea while we wait."

"Yes," said Mary Catherine.

Her eyes followed Anne Marie's movements only half

attending as Anne Marie placed the black kettle over the fire. With her back turned toward Mary Catherine, Anne Marie said something she didn't quite grasp.

"What, Annie?"

"I say, Esther'll never understand."

"She doesn't, that's sure," she returned, not sure what she agreed to. What wouldn't Esther understand? The thought tumbled round and round in her mind, not making sense atall.

"I'm sorry, Annie. What is it she wouldn't understand?"

"The starvin'."

A short, harsh laugh escaped Mary Catherine's lips.

"No, she'd never understand that."

Erupting with mirthless laughter, the cacophony echoing off the walls, Mary Catherine and Annie stopped abruptly upon hearing the slightest creak of a board outside. Holding their breath the women watched as the door opened revealing Jack, standing in his own doorway, clothes blackened and stiff.

"There's no more news," he stated.

Mary Catherine rose to go.

"You're welcome to stay," said Jack.

His face streaked with coal dust held eyes sunken and shadowed with weariness.

"No, I must go home," said Mary Catherine. "If one of the children wakes, I must be there."

Annie hugged her and gave her a kiss on the cheek, smiling encouragement to her.

Mary Catherine crossed over the path and turned once to see her friend gazing after her. She picked her way along the rough path to her own door half a rood away. Lifting the latch, she strained for a sign that the children still slept. In the stillness she decried their even breathing and slipped into the cabin without a sound, closing the door behind her. The glow of dying embers

BRIDGET   Johnson

drew her to the hearth. She pulled a chair close, sat and stirred the coals, added bits, and again stoked them. Removing her shoes, she leaned back in the chair, raising her feet to the stool near the hearth. The tiny flame warmed her toes.

Annie was right about the starving. Esther would never understand that. Losing children Esther could grasp though hers weren't dead. For they were gone to war and could die any day. It takes as much strength in a woman to lose them either way. There was something about Esther. She may not have suffered the same trials as they, but there was a strength about her and a certain brightness. Yes, she brings a glow into a room, and it isn't just her hair.

Mary Catherine wondered why she seemed to draw people of such strength about her. Even Michael. What she had always liked about him was just that. Not just his considerable physical prowess, but that she could lean on him in her own need and he on

BRIDGET — Johnson

her. Reflecting on these things brought her a bit of comfort.

Michael, my strength, don't leave me now. Come home to me, her heart yearned.

Michael it was who had come in from the field one day with an announcement. She recalled their own Sean had been about a year and a half then. Spring of 1850 it was.

So much had happened since Sean's birth. During his first year, hope had come again and for good reason. Not the entire potato crop had rotted that year. But there had been fewer hands to do the planting. The starvation had brought sickness. The fever had taken her father and one of Michael's brothers. There had been no proper wakes because of the starving. But there had been grieving enough. They had been lucky to get them mass prayed and underground. Others had not fared so well. The rent had gone unpaid from both households as they struggled to stay alive.

"Mary Catherine, we have to go," said Michael.

BRIDGET

"Go where, Michael?"

"I'm not sure. America, I think."

A little fear, a little excitement with a bit of hope thrown in for spice simmered within her breast, the sauces of life.

"Will it be better there?"

"I don't know," Michael said. "But nothin' can be as bad as this."

Mary Catherine hesitated, remembering the dying ones she had nursed who had also looked forward to going to America. Some saw neither homeland nor dream.

"Mary Catherine," said Michael. "some of us has to go, so there'll be enough for the rest."

"You're right," Mary Catherine said. "Besides, it's best for the children."

"Children? Whose children?"

"Ours, silly."

BRIDGET

"You're not…."

"I am."

The heat of excitement in his eyes burned its way to the very center of her. Swept off her feet by his embrace, she felt herself lifted and whirled about till she became dizzy. When her toes touched the earth she clung to him, for her head spun.

"We'll go for the sake of the children," she whispered, her face turned up to his.

BRIDGET

BRIDGET

CHAPTER IX

Kinfolk and neighbors of those to be lost to the emigration held a wake that spring in the Cork village square to mourn their going. Bringing food and drink to share, the emigrants and those they were forsaking danced far into the night to the fiddler's tunes. The keening of the strings pierced Mary Catherine's soul, for she knew there was little chance of seeing their loved ones again in this life.

BRIDGET Johnson

    A few days later the emigrants sailed their misty way across the Irish Sea to Liverpool on a crowded ferry. Mary Catherine, familiar with the English seaport having been there before, bent her attention on the ragged crowds on the docks most of whom were Irish and owned only the clothes upon their back. Some, such as themselves, carried a box or a small trunk with their precious few belongings. Food provided by the ship's company she had heard would be in short supply. Not depending on anyone to furnish her husband and son with the means to survive the voyage, Mary Catherine had stored bread along with rough sacks of oatmeal and cornmeal, scrounged from family and neighbors willing to part with what little they possessed. These provisions she carried in her gray shawl slung over her back. They might be a long time at sea, and she'd not see her family go hungry.

    After purchasing their passage tickets Michael found them temporary shelter in an abandoned storehouse for the night, much

BRIDGET   Johnson

like the warehouse in which she had nursed those poor wretches only a few years back. Once settled, she studied the other passengers intending to sail on the ship. Her trained eyes spotted telltale signs of illness, the dark around the eyes, listlessness, and the sweats.

"Michael, are the sick ones goin' on the ship?" Mary Catherine asked.

"There's an inspector," said Michael. "He'll winnow them out. Don't fret so."

Torn between sympathy and dread, still she worried.

Michael then added, "The American's, I've heard, are stricter with their shippin' laws than the English."

"Good," said Mary Catherine. "Sickness in close quarters is deadly."

In the morning they scurried along the wharf to board the waiting rowboats. The ship's crew, shouting the foulest language at the passengers, ferried them to the ship. Never having been abused this way before, Mary Catherine, although offended, resolved to ignore such coarseness.

In the first days after leaving port many people on board suffered with seasickness. Michael and Sean, showing no ill effects, went on deck frequently. Not sure whether the ship or the unborn baby caused her illness, Mary Catherine stayed below to be near the slop-pot in which she retched often in those early days at sea.

Eleven souls shared the cabin with Mary Catherine and her family. Bunks lined the walls, and all belongings were stuffed under the lower ones. In one corner sat a bucket of convenience screened by a woman's shawl, hung for modesty's sake.

Also down with seasickness and occupying a berth together were McGinty's twin girls, not yet sixteen. The oldest son of the third family, Liam, suffered from the dread malady only too familiar to Mary Catherine.

"Mrs. O'Dillon, may I be of some help? I've some nursing experience," she said one day, lifting herself onto her elbow.

"I couldn't impose."

"I must be gettin' up anyway," said Mary Catherine, rising from her bed. "Layin' here won't make me feel better."

"I would like a breath of fresh air, if you're sure you wouldn't mind?"

"Go now. I'll sit with Liam for awhile."

The woman exited the room in a whisht. The door, only a curtain on a rope, flapped about in the wake of her going. Seating herself on a box near the boy, Mary Catherine stroked his flushed brow, while the smell of his fetid breath confirmed her suspicions.

"Liam, look at me," said Mary Catherine.

Obeying in his delirium, the boy turned his head toward her

and opened his eyes. The glassy stare alleviated her concern not one whit. Near the shawled corner stood a small table with a seawater cask braced against a tottering leg. Mary Catherine, ladled some of the brackish liquid from the barrel into the cracked washbowl that sat on the table and returned with it to the boy. Then she took the rag his mother had been using and gently sponged his face. He moaned and, clutching her by the wrist, held her hand to his brow. Removing his fingers one by one till he let loose, Mary Catherine continued to bathe him.

A little later Mrs. O'Dillon returned, stopping just inside the cabin. Mary Catherine motioned for the woman to come close. The face before her changed from one of concern to distress. She hurried to Mary Catherine's side.

"What is it?" said Mrs. O'Dillon.

"I think he's got the ship's fever," Mary Catherine said. "Road fever we called it at home."

BRIDGET

"I feared it might be more than seasickness. What am I to do?"

"Cool the fever. Otherwise keep him warm," said Mary Catherine, placing her hand on the woman's arm. "And try to get him to drink a little tea."

"Is there medicine for it?"

"I don't know. You'll have to ask the captain if he has anything in his ship's stores that would be of use."

Mrs. O'Dillon sat with the boy, freeing Mary Catherine to go above deck.

"Are you all right?" Michael said, taking her hand as she appeared topside. "Should you be up?"

"I feel stronger movin' about."

Supporting her with his arm around her waist, Michael led her to a covered hatch. There Mary Catherine sat down hard as the ship lurched up then down the swells. The sea looked angry to her

BRIDGET   Johnson

in its seamless gray of sky and deep as it tossed the ship up one watery hill and down another. What amazed her was that the ship's complement actually expected to stay afloat long enough to sight land. This idea didn't even alarm her, which surprised her even more.

Grilles were set up by the ship's crew in a long, narrow row on the deck. The passengers lined up along both sides, bent over the wood fire, cooked their bits of salted pork, and fried their cakes. After several others had finished Mary Catherine took her place on the line, mixed a ration of cornmeal from the ship's stores with seawater, and cooked some cakes for her own family.

Having finished their meal, she and her family sat on one of the hatches, when water rained down from the shrouds onto the grilles hissing out the coals. Steam mingling with cries of vexation rose from those still engaged in cooking their food. Mary Catherine looked up into the ship's rigging to see a face

BRIDGET   Johnson

sneering down. A crooked nose, no doubt broken in a brawl, marred a countenance already deformed by a scar that snaked down the man's sun-darkened cheek. Then and there she vowed to be first on the cooking line so as not to get caught by one such as he.

The following day in the mid-afternoon the wind came up, and the sky leadened once more. The passengers had been allowed only a few minutes on deck that morning. The sky and the sea merged into one dark living thing, enveloping the small brig, intent on devouring them all.

"Get below, all a'ya!"

The first mate scowled as he delivered his scathing blast. They obeyed in an instant, scrambling down the ladders. Unwashed bodies cramped together soon thickened the air below deck. The slop pot couldn't be emptied, intensifying the stench of vomit, excrement, and urine, strangling the occupants, invading their hair, clothing, even the very walls. Several days passed before the storm abated and they were allowed up to breathe deep draughts of salt air. More passengers took sick. Some like Liam had contracted the fever. Mrs. O'Dillon shared her son's berth, her face and hands mushrooming to twice their natural size. Mary Catherine with Michael's help did what they could to bring comfort to the stricken. The McGinty twins appeared quite thin and weak.

"Michael, there must be something more to be done."

"You shouldn't be doin' this a'tall."

"We have to do something," said Mary Catherine.

"You should be thinkin' about the babe," Michael said. "You might catch it yourself."

"As long as I'm closed in here, I might get it. What would you have me do? Jump overboard?"

The shock of her words, she marked, brought a tightness to

his jaw. Mary Catherine wished she'd kept her tongue for she knew he meant well. Anger darkened his eyes.

"I'm sorry, Michael. I didn't mean it that way."

"What way might that be?"

"I'm not blamin' you, Michael, for our comin', but I just can't leave them to fend for themselves."

"Leave well enough alone," he said and, turning his back to her, bolted from the room.

She yearned to run after him, but instead Mary Catherine turned from the door through which he had vanished and gazed upon the sick who lay in their beds. *And if I don't care for them, Michael, who will?*

BRIDGET

CHAPTER X

"I'm sorry, Love, that I brought you to this."

Mary Catherine wakened to Michael's touch as he bathed her face and then her arms. Focusing, hmind registered the fear betrayed by his eyes.

"You didn't," she whispered. "I wished to come."

Why did she whisper she asked herself. Hadn't she the strength to speak out? She tried to raise her head and found it too heavy. She quit the struggle and succumbed to oblivion.

BRIDGET

When next she woke, alone, Michael's not being there confused her.

"Michael," Mary Catherine called out as she scanned the room.

She thought it had to be her own voice she heard. Maybe it was all a dream. She convinced herself she'd waken soon, yet still remained perplexed.

Then Michael's face appeared before her.

"Are you really here, Michael?"

"I'm here, Love."

"Where's Sean?"

"He's about," said Michael. "Be quiet now. Rest."

Shades of the dead grabbed at her, pulling her down, and seized hold of her arms and legs. Visages of the dying from the hospital knitted up with the faces of father, brother, and the starving along the road became embroiled in her imaginings.

BRIDGET   Johnson

Bodies piled like stones on top one another in carts and against the hedges near the road. Leave me be, she screamed at them. You can't have me.

Rolling from side to side, Mary Catherine clung to her berth, her life raft. Finally the tempest ceased. Once more in safe harbor she rested. When next she woke her eyes were encrusted. In the dim light that shone from the single porthole Mary Catherine peered round the cabin through half-stuck eyelids at her fellow voyagers as they still slept. She must rise. The arm she willed to support this effort refused her command. Trying her leg, she fared no better. I'm alive, aren't I?

"Mummy, are you awake?"

The concerned countenance of little Sean hovered near her.

"Yes, Sean, but I can't seem to get myself goin'."

"Da – Da, Mummy's awake."

In an instant Michael swung down from the bunk above to

her side.

"Welcome back, darlin' girl."

"What do you mean?"

"You've been ill, very ill."

"Michael, is that why I can't move?" said Mary Catherine. "I can't lift my head."

"It's been a while since you were last on your feet."

"How long?"

"About two weeks."

Two weeks?

"Help me up, Michael."

"Are you sure?"

"Yes," she said.

Michael pulled a low stool close and, grasping her under her arms, struggled to lift her upright onto it. Once she was seated he held her there. Glad of his strength Mary Catherine bent her attention on exploring her parts. Touching her chest she ran her hands along her ribs, too prominent now. Then she passed her hands down over her waist and gasped.

"Steady now, my girl," came Michael's command, his voice rasping in her ears.

Taking one of her hands, he raised it to his lips and kissed her palm.

"Michael, where's my baby?"

"Gone, Love."

Too much, Mary Catherine cried in her heart. I want to go home. Take me home. Oh, dear Blessed Mother. She couldn't bear this. Not now.

"It's gone to be with your brother, Sean, and your father."

Looking into his eyes, Mary Catherine probed the grief now living there.

"Michael."

BRIDGET   Johnson

She could say no more for the pain of it overtook her. Pressing herself against him, Mary Catherine searched for comfort in Michael's arms. Together they rocked and rocked in their sorrow.

BRIDGET

CHAPTER XI

In another week Mary Catherine became strong enough to once again go up on deck. Could it be her imagination, or were some faces missing?"

"Where are the McGinty twins?" she said.

"They died of the fever," said Michael.

"And, Liam?"

"Him, too."

BRIDGET   Johnson

Hearing this news, Mary Catherine slumped against Michael as he supported her with his arm.

"Mrs. O'Dillon's still abed," he said. "Her husband died, too."

"Poor woman."

"She still has Bridy and Ben," said Michael.

Mary Catherine spied Mr. McGinty, the father of the twins, standing at the rail of the foredeck, staring out to sea.

"Michael, shouldn't we say something?"

"Would it do any good?" said Michael. "He's lost just about all a man can. First his wife at the hospital in Liverpool and now his children."

"But we must, Michael," said Mary Catherine.

They moved toward the man, and she placed her hand on his arm. He turned to her, but the sadness in his eyes allowed no one to enter there. He turned again to the sea. Mary Catherine stood silent, patting his arm, and doubted he even felt her touch.

More passengers died, their shrouded bodies often dropped clandestinely into the sea at night. On the rare day when the weather and Captain Bathpoole permitted, the captain would read a somber blessing over the dead before dispatching their bodies to the deep and their souls to eternity.

The day dawned bright, and a stiff wind carried the ship forward when Mary Catherine learned that Mr. McGinty had disappeared during the night.

"It's a sin and a shame that this morning is so gay," said Michael.

Mary Catherine, letting the remark pass, touched Sean's dark curls. Then holding tight to Sean's hand, Mary Catherine strolled the deck with her husband and her son.

"Mummy, I won't blow away," Sean said. "Must you hang onto me so?"

BRIDGET

Releasing her hold on her son, Mary Catherine felt cast adrift from him. She looked at little Sean and believed that in some strange way he had grown older on this journey. As Mary Catherine watched, entranced, she soon glimpsed Sean skipping about amongst the crew working on the deck.

Although Mary Catherine had never before questioned Michael's decision to leave Eire, she wondered if they had accomplished anything by coming away? Shrugging her shoulders, she figured there was nothing for it now but to accept it. McGinty hadn't.

All sails billowed in the blustery breeze, the journey almost over according to the reckoning of the ship's crew. A squall blew in from the horizon in blackening clouds, dashing the raging seas over and under them, and sending passengers below. The ship strove for its life every timber complaining loudly of the strain, while waves crashed against the hull and below deck the three of

BRIDGET

them huddled together, riding the bucking floor. Up they went on some wild ride, then down into the valleys of the sea. Between the wails of the torrent Mary Catherine heard children crying and the voices of mother or father trying to soothe them. Some children, motherless and fatherless, had no one to comfort them and sobbed unabated.

The sadness in Mary Catherine deepened within her. The weeping children sounded the depths of her own grief for the lost babe, too dreadful for tears.

The storm lasted for three days. When it ceased they were becalmed on a glass sea of endless silken azure. The captain tacked the ship, trying to catch each wayward stirring breath. Rationing both food and water, the austere captain, it was rumored, saved larger portions of both for his crew, while the passengers' own food stores ran thin. Everyone had accepted this practice in the past. Now the men's grumbling became strident.

BRIDGET   Johnson

"Mary Catherine, don't come on deck today," said Michael.

A warm zephyr had sprung up, coaxing her to go above to the open sea air.

"And why not?" she said. "It seems a fair enough day."

His eyes would not meet hers as she questioned him. Her lethargy of weeks past left her, alarm clearing the fog from her mind.

"What is bein' planned, Michael?" she asked.

He did not answer.

"Tell me!"

"It's best you don't know," said Michael. "Take care of the boy."

For a moment he stood in the doorway with his back to her; then he left the cabin without so much as a glance in her direction. Present now in mind and body, Mary Catherine clasped Sean's hand so tightly that he squealed. Wrapping her arms about him she crushed him close, listening for sounds. She sat on the bunk, her son curled up in her lap, waiting. A muffled explosion brought her to her feet, straining to heed the slightest sound. Had someone fired a cannon? Daggers of horror pricked every part of her while she clutched Sean's hand. Then she heard the racket of heavy feet stumbling down the steps from topside, and Michael's downcast face appeared as he pushed the curtain aside. Relief flooded her. Dropping the boy's hand, she threw herself upon her husband.

"Mary, Mother of God! Praised be you're all right."

She led him to the cot, clinging to his hand as he sat down upon it.

"What were you thinkin'?"

"We needed the food for our families," Michael said matter-of-factly. "The captain and crew would not give it to us without a fight, would they now?"

"Was anyone hurt?"

BRIDGET   Johnson

"No. They fired the cannon to scare us off."

Staying below, they nibbled on bits of fried cornbread that they had hoarded, for the captain allowed no one up as punishment. After two days they were permitted up out of their holes. Nervous as moles they blinked in the brilliant sunlight, and their tongues soon loosened, and the gossip flowed.

"The extra food didn't keep the first mate well, did it now?" said McGuire. "He died just as quick, even though well-fed."

"Too bad about McGinty jumpin'."

No one had said it out loud before, but all had known.

"Two more of the dead dumped last night."

Mary Catherine listened as she bent over the grill. With the morning's small ration of flour and corn meal she mixed and fried cakes for Sean, Michael, and herself.

"How long's it been now? Three months?"

"Seems like."

A scent borne to Mary Catherine on the salt air struck her as familiar. She looked to the west. Nothing but foam capped rolling seas there. She breathed deeply. Could she be mistaken?

BRIDGET

CHAPTER XII

"Mummy, - Mummy?"

A small hand tugged at her shawl, and the coal black of Michael's own eyes gazed at her from Fiona's eight-year-old face.

Mary Catherine's unshod feet had chilled to ice while the fire had turned to ashes. Rising from the chair where she had slept the night, she glanced toward the children's beds. Seeing their slumbering forms, she scanned the doorway to the room where her

BRIDGET

own bed stood, coverlet undisturbed. She poked among the dying embers on the hearth and found some still glowed. Blowing them to life, Mary Catherine added some sticks and a few coal bits gleaned from the culm banks.

Gathering Fiona onto her lap, she settled back in the rocking chair with her child, who snuggled down to warm herself. Then Mary Catherine sent up a prayer that Michael might be found alive and embraced the quiet of the moment.

Behind her Mary Catherine heard a bed creak and, looking round, saw Sean's dark head emerge from under the blanket. She nodded to him.

Coming close he said, "Mother, I'm goin' to the mines. They'll have need of me."

"Must you?"

Sean's steadfast blue eyes looked into hers.

"The mules won't wait to be fed. Brownie needs me."

BRIDGET   Johnson

Mary Catherine knew the truth of what he said. Animals don't care for themselves. What she wanted to say, but could not bring herself to, was that she had need of him now. They spoke no more of it. Sean went to the trunk by his bed, took out a clean pair of trousers, and put them on.

"Sean, come take your sister," Mary Catherine said. "I'll not have you goin' to the mines hungry."

Putting a kettle over the fire, she sliced some bread for his lunch, then cooked the breakfast mush.

"I'll take Fiona now," she said. "Sean, you go and get some milk from Lady."

Sean took a wooden bucket and left the cabin, returning in a few minutes with it half full.

"That cow is worth her weight," said Mary Catherine, saying what she said every morning. She knew it. But the ritual created some semblance of normalcy in her life, and she clung to the habit, her lifeboat in her own personal storm.

"Up, children," Mary Catherine called. "Time for breakfast."

Her brood stumbled toward her, rubbing sleep from their eyes. Patrick and Rose dragged their chairs from their post by the wall to the table, which stood halfway between beds and hearth.

"Sean, say the prayer," said Mary Catherine.

"Thank you, Father, for what we have received from Thy bounty," Sean murmured. "And, Lord, bring our da safe home."

"Sean," cried Mary Catherine, who had shrunk from telling the younger ones about the disaster in the mine.

Four young faces turned to her for an answer to the unspoken question.

"Your father still works in the mine and hasn't come home as yet," Mary Catherine said.

"Why hasn't he come home?" asked Rose, her bronze curls

bouncing as her head swung from Sean to Mary Catherine.

Sean gulped down his mush and said, "I have to go now, Mother." Then sticking a slice of bread in his mouth and taking his coat from a peg by the door, he turned and said, "If I find out anything, I'll come for you."

She and the children finished their meal in a silence pricked through with discomfort.

"Catherine Marie, gather up the dishes," Mary Catherine said, trying to keep her tone cheerful. "The rest of you straighten up your beds and your clothes."

Once the shanty reflected an acceptable order and cleanliness, Mary Catherine called her children to her by the hearth.

"Tell us a story," demanded Rose.

"Tell us about comin' to America, Mummy," added Fiona.

Patrick crawled up onto her lap, his ebony eyes questioning

her hesitation. Sadness sat on her heart, but she must distract them from the grave truth sure to come.

"Please, Mummy," said Patrick.

"Please, Mummy, tell us," said Rose.

"You've heard the story many times before," said Mary Catherine.

"Again, Mummy, again," pleaded Patrick.

Looking into their faces, dear to her, tears blurred her vision for a moment. Then she began…, "Sean was a little'un, when we sailed for America.…"

BRIDGET

CHAPTER XIII

"Land ho!" had come the call from the shrouds on their last day at sea.

They glided over the water following a path glowing golden in the setting sun. Unlike any harbor Mary Catherine had seen before, buildings seemed to rise out of the water, crowding in on each other as if to see which could get a closer look at the newcomers. The ship dropped anchor, and they waited for word to disembark. No word came that night.

In the morning Mary Catherine, her family, and the other

passengers who were fit scrubbed themselves and their quarters in excited anticipation. And they waited.

Quarantined they were, according to the captain. To be kept aboard till they could be medically examined. "The new country doesn't want any of your diseases."

At the end of the day Captain Bathpoole growled, "Get your slops cooked. You'll not be inspected today, I've been told."

"Maybe tomorrow," said one man.

"Yes, tomorrow," echoed a woman's voice.

Two days later the health inspector arrived, and excited immigrants crowded around him.

"Any dead on board?" asked the doctor. "Sick?"

"No dead today," said Captain Bathpoole. "Last one was buried at sea a day out."

"Show me the sick," the physician demanded.

The first mate took him below deck, and within ten minutes

they reappeared. The immigrants awaited the doctor's verdict in agitated and sullen silence.

"We'll send a ferry for the well," said the doctor. "Then we'll dispose of the sick aboard."

With that statement the health inspector clambered over the side and was gone.

Again they waited. No one came. Food stores ran out. Mary Catherine's family had only crumbs to nibble on that night and went to bed hungry.

A couple of days later the ferry came just before dawn. Michael shouldered their wooden trunk, while Mary Catherine hoisted her shawl over her shoulder, making a sling of it in which to carry their smalls. Shifting the bundle to one side, she carried Sean on her other hip. The ferry deposited them in the shadow of a fort-like building, where the immigrants crowded through a cavernous opening like so many cattle herded into a barn.

BRIDGET — Johnson

"Mary Catherine," Michael whispered in a hoarse voice. "Take my hand. We'll not be goin' in there."

Pressing along docks choked with men carrying cargo boxes and barrels in every direction, Michael pulled her first this way then the other in the crush of bodies. Mary Catherine feared their hands would be torn apart, and she would be lost with Sean in this strange city, if city it be. Holding fast as he dragged her forward, Mary Catherine couldn't see where they were going.

A loud concussion shook the earth beneath her feet. They had heard this same explosion at dawn each day when aboard ship. Captain Bathpoole had explained that it was the custom in New York City to greet the sun each morning with cannon shot. Still Mary Catherine clung to Michael's reassuring grasp.

No longer jostled and elbowed about, she looked up at dark walls, dwarfing her from both sides of the street. Buildings leaning so close, they blended with the gray sky and painted a

BRIDGET   Johnson

dismal scene. The clouds overhead darkened with the burden of rain, and Mary Catherine felt sure they would soon relieve themselves of their moisture. With that a cool drop stroked her cheek.

"Sit here, Mary Catherine."

"Where are you goin'?"

"I have to find us shelter," said Michael. "I'll be back quick enough,"

"Hurry," Mary Catherine murmured in a voice only audible to herself, for she wouldn't weigh him down with her fears.

Huddled on the trunk Michael had dropped from his shoulder, Mary Catherine clasped Sean close and covered him with her shawl and her body, one large lump piled on the side of the road. Rain dribbled down her back, chilling her spine, forcing her to crouch even lower. Her body sodden Mary Catherine peered into the curtain of wet, staring down the dim alley into which

Michael had vanished.

"I've found a place," announced Michael's weary voice from behind her.

She followed him down the muddy ruts and around a corner to another street that looked the same. If she ever had to find her way about, Mary Catherine doubted she could. A few more steps and Michael led her through a door and up two flights of stairs. At the end of a dark hall he opened a door.

The gray outside seeped through dirty and broken panes from a single window at the far end of the room. In the center stood a table bereft of chairs. Along one wall she saw cots, and near another wall bedding rolls rested on the floor. Michael pointed to an uninhabited wall. The room appeared more Spartan than the cabin on the ship. For here no beds were provided, not even planks. The three McNurneys shuffled along the wall on their right to the space that seemed free for the taking.

BRIDGET   Johnson

Pitching the trunk onto the floor against the wall, Michael bade her sit on it.

"Mary Catherine, I need to seek something for us to sleep on."

"Now, Michael?"

"What better time?"

Impatience infused discord in every word he spoke, and she heard it.

"All right, Michael," said Mary Catherine. "But, please, be quick."

He had disappeared out the door before she had finished speaking.

Once accustomed to the gloom, she spied a small, black stove at the far end of the room near the lone window. Inspecting the rest of the place, Mary Catherine noticed two dark pair of eyes staring back at her from one of the bundles against the opposite

BRIDGET   Johnson

wall.

Holding the sleeping Sean in her arms, Mary Catherine watched as the bundle moved, and two small figures scrambled out and waddled toward her. Poor little ones, the rags hanging on their bodies couldn't hide their bulging stomachs. Sure signs of starvation she knew. As Mary Catherine gazed at them, she envisioned the bodies piled like so much cord wood along the country roads of Erin. Wretched babies with distended bellies lying lifeless, hand in hand with brother, sister, mother, or father.

The tears coursed down her cheeks, interrupted by a movement again in the bundle across the room. A figure rose.

"Kevin, Eileen, back here."

The voice sharp and cross, the utterance hardly human. When the creature stood, its unkempt garment proclaimed its owner woman. The woman snatched the waifs up and dragged them back to their bundle.

BRIDGET

Michael returned with clean straw, and she spread her shawl upon it. Soon they slept cupped in each others arms with Sean between them, their stomachs painfully empty.

In the following days Michael scrounged for bed and bedding. Then he ran a rope from beam to beam, hanging a blanket from it, giving them a semblance of privacy. Michael found work laboring on the docks and exchanged the little money he earned for bread and potatoes.

One day as she cooked potato soup on the stove, Mary Catherine noticed Kevin and Eileen creeping ever closer.

"Sean, say hello," Mary Catherine said.

Sean hung back, hands clasped tightly behind his back.

"Come close, little ones," said Mary Catherine.

They shuffled nearer. The boy cocked his head and squinted at her.

"Would you like a taste of my soup, Kevin?" she said.

"I would," said Kevin.

The children squatted in front of her and opened their mouths. Ladling a small amount into a bowl, she spooned the broth into their mouths, poor little birds.

"Where is your mother?" said Mary Catherine.

Eileen swallowed a mouthful and said, "I don't know."

"Lookin' for work," Kevin explained.

"She'd leave you alone?"

"We're not alone," Kevin said defiantly. "We're together."

The door to the room crashed back against the wall.

"Leave me kids be."

Mary Catherine stared at the woman's angry face.

"You think I can't feed me own?"

Shock and frenzied fury battled for supremacy within Mary Catherine. This woman attacked her for providing food for the little ragamuffins. She wished to hurl back a scathing reply, but compressed her lips with great effort and denied her tongue that liberty. Instead Mary Catherine turned her back on the woman and stared out the window, willing calmness on her soul. Taking the kettle and Sean behind their blanket, she fed her child and afterwards laid him down for a nap.

Then filling the bowl with more broth, Mary Catherine crossed the room again.

"I'm sorry if I offended you in some way," she said to the woman.

The woman sat, her back against the wall.

"Why are you bein' kind to me?"

Mary Catherine recognized the suspicion in her voice. Starting to turn back, the woman's voice arrested her in mid step.

"Why?"

Now, instead of suspicion, she heard fear.

Facing her, Mary Catherine examined the woman. The

face appeared thin. Probably fed her children before herself. Framing the pinched features, hung stringy unclean hair, the color of which couldn't be determined. But when she lifted her head to look full upon Mary Catherine, the green eyes betrayed the youth that lingered in her being.

Sitting down on the floor cross-legged, Mary Catherine looked from the sleeping children to their mother.

"I could not deny the hunger in their eyes," Mary Catherine said.

The face before her softened a bit.

"You would do me a kindness to taste the soup," Mary Catherine said, holding out the steaming bowl.

With shaking hands the woman took the bowl from her and supped.

"I cannot repay you," she said when she had finished the meal.

BRIDGET   Johnson

"A small prayer will do."

Mary Catherine hesitated putting the next question, it being a bit intrusive.

"Do you have a husband?"

"I had," she said. "He died on the way over."

Mary Catherine had long wondered, when watching bodies being committed to the deep, what became of those belonging to such people? This is what happened to them.

"What is your name, if you don't mind my askin'?"

"Kathleen," she said with spirit. "Kathleen Danaher."

"Well, Kathleen Danaher, I have a thought," said Mary Catherine. "Know that I'll be watchin' your children while you look for work. That should give you some peace of mind."

Tears spilled down Kathleen's face.

"No time for tears now," said Mary Catherine. Then the spark of an idea fired her imagination. "I know. Let's wash your hair."

Before Kathleen could protest, Mary Catherine fetched the bucket from her corner of the room, splashed some water into a kettle, and set it to warm on the stove. After washing and brushing Kathleen's hair, Mary Catherine lit a stub of candle as twilight dimmed the room. She then brought the candle and Kathleen to the grimy window, where candle-glow reflected hints of scarlet in the girl's long tresses.

"Oh," gasped Kathleen.

"Oh, indeed," said Mary Catherine. "You'll be right enough now."

BRIDGET

CHAPTER XIV

A brother and sister, Francis and Moira Rafferty, occupied another wall of the none too spacious room. Mary Catherine saw little of them, for the lucky ones worked. Francis had a job on the docks the same as Michael. His sister worked as maid to an Irish family that had been in America for more than one generation. Moira had informed Mary Catherine that this family had acquired property.

"Enough to hang lace curtains in the window," said Moira.

BRIDGET

"Do they work you hard?" asked Mary Catherine.

"Hard enough. They say I'm treated as one of the family. I've a family, thank you very much. And have no need of another. Not the likes of them anyway."

Moira had expressed her thoughts more than once to Mary Catherine. Listening patiently, not even sure she wanted such confidences, Mary Catherine absorbed bits and pieces of American ways.

"Would you think of that."

The apartment door crashed back upon the wall as Moira burst through it. Coming to a stop to catch her breath, she planted her hands firmly on her hips.

"Calmly, Moira. Here, sit," said Mary Catherine, patting a stool near her.

"Sit I can't."

The young woman had recently left her position with the

BRIDGET   Johnson

Irish family to take a more lucrative one with a wealthy Protestant family uptown. Striding first up the room and then down, Moira paused in front of Mary Catherine.

"Come, Moira, what has you so upset?"

"She called me Bridget."

Mary Catherine clapped her hand over her mouth.

"You might well be astounded," said Moira.

More amused than amazed Mary Catherine struggled with the hilarity that threatened to engulf her, swallowed hard, lowered her hand to her lap, and looked up at Moira.

"Why would she call you that now?"

"Says it's easier than tryin' to remember all us Irish girls' names. Confuses her it does."

"It's a nice enough name," said Mary Catherine.

"But it's not me own."

"Is the pay good?"

"It's good enough," Moira said.

"Well then," said Mary Catherine.

The lines of anger around Moira's mouth softened, and she sat down on the stool.

"Could I give you a cup of tea, Moira?"

"That would be nice indeed."

When not listening to Moira's complaints, Mary Catherine looked after Kathleen's little ones, while she sought work. Added to that, most days she washed clothes, scrubbing them on a washboard Michael had scavenged. Then Mary Catherine strung them up on a rope the length of the room to dry. On occasion she asked Mrs. McLaren in the apartment next door to watch the children, while she went hunting food from the street vendors.

On Sundays Michael took his family to a wood a few blocks away with Kathleen and her children tagging along. In a clearing some Irish and others too poor to pay rent in the tenement

BRIDGET

buildings had pitched tents or had built packing box shanties to shelter their families. Michael strode off to where a few of the men sat on upturned buckets. Mary Catherine spread her shawl on the ground for Kathleen and herself to sit upon, while the children chased rings around them.

"You know," said Kathleen. "I got a position at the mill."

"Have you now?" Mary Catherine said. "And is it hard work you'll be doin'?"

"Hard enough. We'll be sewin' clothes and expected to make a quota."

"What is that?"

"We'll only be paid for finished pieces," said Moira. "The faster you are, the more you earn."

"I suppose you'll be the grand lady with so much money."

"I don't think so. It takes many pieces to add up to even a small wage, I hear."

BRIDGET

"Well then, don't you be lettin' them work you to death," said Mary Catherine. "You'll not be much use to your children if you're gone now, will you?"

"Speakin' of them," said Moira. "I'll be workin' long hours."

"Kathleen, don't worry so. Did I not say I'd watch over them?"

Kathleen laid her hand on Mary Catherine's as a tear slipped down the girl's cheek, baptizing their hands.

Not being able to abide the blasphemies she heard from both men and women in the tenements, when a pleasant day presented itself Mary Catherine and the children escaped to the park. What good would it do to blame the Lord? It wouldn't put food on the table.

One morning, glad that Michael had already left for the docks, Mary Catherine felt the familiar pain. One thing she knew,

BRIDGET

it was too soon.

"Children, come. Mrs. McLaren will care for you this mornin'."

Gripping Sean's hand, Mary Catherine pushed Kevin and Eileen before her. She hesitated only for a second as the pain drove her on. Having rapped on Mrs. McLaren's door, it slowly opened, and Mary Catherine shoved the children ahead of her into the room.

"Mrs. McLaren, could you watch the little ones?" said Mary Catherine. "I have an urgent errand to run."

It wasn't really a lie, she reasoned. Child birth being an urgent matter at best.

The shawled, white head nodded, and with that assent Mary Catherine pulled the door shut and hurried back to their room. Then going to the cot behind the blanket, Mary Catherine had one

BRIDGET

hand on the bed and one on the concealing drape when the pain knifed through her lower body. Her legs, weakened with the onslaught, buckled beneath her.

She bit her lip and tasted the salted warmth of blood in her mouth. Groaning, Mary Catherine twisted the bedclothes in her hands and rested her head on the tick as the torture increased.

"Please, God, help me," Mary Catherine prayed in a whisper during a moment of surcease. "Dear Blessed Mother, have pity on me."

Having sensed that she was with child but a month before, she hadn't told Michael. A baby lost on the ship and now this. No, she hadn't been able to tell him. Shudders wracked her body, but she tried not to cry out, for then someone would come, and he would know. The pains finally stopped. Exhausted, Mary Catherine gathered up the unrecognizable lump from the floor where it had dropped and enfolded it in her black waist, thinking it

BRIDGET

fitting as a shroud. She then cleansed herself and scrubbed every trace of blood from the floor. Resting for a moment on the edge of the cot, she then braced herself and stood, wrapped her shawl about her, and tenderly covered the bundle she held in her arms.

Hugging it to her, Mary Catherine stumbled down the stairs and out into the crowded street. Wending her way betwixt the scurrying bodies near her, she passed through the jostle of humans unnoticed. She walked heedless of direction, in the end finding herself in the park where they had gone of a Sunday. Avoiding the tents and shanties, Mary Catherine sought anonymity among the trees and shrubs. Hidden in the denseness of the wood she crouched against a towering oak.

She then took a spoon from a pocket in her skirt, and scraped at the frozen ground. The effort brought forth tears, which spilled down into the dirt. This patch of earth had not been disturbed before. Mary Catherine felt grateful for this small blessing. For it meant that her child would not be trod on. Her babe would rest in peace. The tears continued to flow, softening the small grave. One alone in the sea, now one alone in this land. Mary Catherine placed her bundle in the hollowed earth and filled it, sifting the soil with her hands as if planting with care a treasured seed. Patting the earth over the mound beneath the tree, she pressed the ground firmly in place. And she prayed.

"Blessed Mother, keep my babes in your arms till I come to hold them in mine."

Another moment of rest, then she must return. Hitching herself up the trunk of the tree, Mary Catherine propped herself against it, then left its strength, pushing herself forward. She lurched, almost collapsing. Shaken, Mary Catherine willed her limbs to carry her onward, treading the ruts with care so as not to fall. In this fashion she made her way into the milieu from which she had come.

BRIDGET

CHAPTER XV

"Did you think I wouldn't know you were with child?"

The anger in Michael's voice grated, and Mary Catherine dared not raise her eyes to his for fear of what she'd read there.

"We're leavin' this dirty city first chance I get," said Michael.

With this declaration she knew that he blamed himself for the infant's death. So Mary Catherine went to him, and he took her into his arms.

BRIDGET   Johnson

Winter soon lifted its icy hand, and Michael said the time had come to make the move. He had heard come spring more men would be needed to work the coal mines in Pennsylvania. Mary Catherine packed their battered wooden trunk, and Michael bound it together with ropes. Early one morning he lifted it upon his shoulder, and Mary Catherine followed without a word, carrying all she could in the shawl she slung over her shoulder. Taking Sean by the hand, she set out with her husband upon the murky dawn streets. They would take the ferry across the Hudson River to New Jersey to catch the train just at sunup, Michael had said. Stumbling over refuse thrown from tenement windows, they plodded along rutted and muddy lanes soggy from slops and wash water that had been flung upon them.

Arriving dockside well before dawn, the stench of the sewage flow engendered gratitude in Mary Catherine that they had refrained from eating that morning. The sky blazed crimson in the

BRIDGET   Johnson

east. But soon clouds crept toward the rising, fiery sphere and blotted it slowly from view. Mist fell upon the crowd gathered on the pier, cooling excitement into discomfort. The dampening chilled Mary Catherine, and Sean's hand in hers trembled with the cold as a raw wind assailed them. Pulling him close into her skirts, she enfolded him in her garment.

"We'll soon be across the river," said Mary Catherine in a soothing voice. "Then you'll be on a train, Sean. Won't that be thrillin'?" she finished with a note of excitement.

"Yes, Mummy."

Sean peeked out from her skirt wrapped round his smiling face, framing his rosy cheeks.

Thrilling for her, too, being her first train ride.

The next moment they were jostled and elbowed as the crowd surged toward the wharf's edge. She lost sight of Michael. Her arm stretched taut, she held onto Sean as they were pulled along by the crush. Then everyone halted. Bunched together. A herd.

Drawing Sean close to her, Mary Catherine caught sight of Michael, struggling to reach them through the glut of bodies.

"Thought I'd lost you sure," he said.

"What was all that about?" said Mary Catherine.

"Oh, someone said we were about to board," said Michael. "And that's all it took."

"Are we boardin' soon?"

In answer to her question the human mass about her shifted. This time they moved forward at a sluggish pace and were driven down a ramp to the open deck of a steamboat. Mary Catherine shuffled through a doorway with her hand on Michael's back as they entered a large room with few seats, and those already taken. Resting on the trunk Michael had put down, Mary Catherine bade Sean sit beside her on the wooden, plank floor.

BRIDGET   Johnson

After a tedious hour a horn blasted, the floor shuddered, and the ferry churned away into deep water. The loading of cargo to go by rail on the other side had caused the delay, Michael had informed her. Bodies crowded against bodies on board the vessel. Mary Catherine fretted about staying afloat with so much human haulage.

Once docked on the far shore the grand rush began in the reverse. The throng charged for the exits and the ramp, bearing her family along. One homogeneous lump of humanity careering headlong toward the train depot. The mist had changed to steady falling rain.

After reaching the station they were given ample time to heed the cold drizzle. Every head turned one way then another. Gathered together, wildly looking about, waiting for the signal to move. It came in a shout.

"All aboard!"

BRIDGET   Johnson

With one fused movement they pressed toward the cars on the siding.

Climbing the iron steps, Mary Catherine entered the car and looked about her, noting the close rows of planks that passed for seats. They squeezed through to one midway in the car, and Michael kicked the trunk under the bench. With Sean between them they perched on the narrow board, seeming built for children not grown men and women.

They sat. They waited. Mary Catherine gazed about the car, other passengers' questioning glances returning her look.

"I'm goin' to see what's the hold-up," said Michael as he rose and headed for the back of the car.

More waiting.

"They're loadin' up," he said upon his return.

"How much longer?" said Mary Catherine.

Michael bent over her to reply.

BRIDGET   Johnson

"Can't tell," he whispered.

Several hours went by.

Mary Catherine had just taken a corn cake from the folds of her shawl and broken it, when short toots from the train's engine sounded. As she was about to give half to Sean the train lurched, bouncing the corn cake out of her hand onto the floor. Accompanied by the hammering of metal on metal, the train then chugged and slipped along the rails. And Sean scrambled after his lunch.

Before long the passengers' chatter consorted with the clacking and hopping of the train along the tracks, resonating to a deafening crescendo. To guard against the jolting and jarring, Mary Catherine braced her feet against the wooden floor lest she be bumped off the bench. Every few miles they stopped to take on wood, water, and more passengers. Overcrowding continued till Mary Catherine imagined the car might well swell up and split its sides.

Around noontime the train stopped for the midday meal. Since they had not the money for foodstuffs, they simply got out to walk and stretch, then returned to the car to share cold boiled potatoes.

"Where will we end up, Michael?" said Mary Catherine.

"We're goin' to somewhere near Allentown in Lehigh County."

"Will this train get us there?"

"This one or another," said Michael. "We'll see."

Mary Catherine took what comfort she could in his vague assurances and decided to enjoy what she could of the trip. After the grim gray of the city, the light green mist that hung about the budding trees giving promise of spring confirmed her dreams and hopes of what America might be. The further away from the city they traveled the more growing things she saw, even a bit of white

BRIDGET   Johnson

and violet from early spring flowers. Mary Catherine found herself eagerly scanning the countryside, searching out the little blooms, a sort of game of hide and seek between herself and God's gifts of field and wood.

The train pulled off onto a siding, stopping near a small settlement. A short time later another train whistled by headed in the opposite direction. So close it came Mary Catherine estimated, if she had stuck her head out the window, it would have been sheared off.

Just as night darkened the landscape they ground to a halt on another siding. The ticket agent told them they'd have to go to the station and purchase their tickets for the next train, which would be boarded in about an hour. Seeing the few coins Michael held in his hand, Mary Catherine wondered if it would be enough to get them through. He left her sitting on the depot boardwalk, returning shortly with passes for the next train.

BRIDGET

"Well?" she asked.

"We'll get there, Mary Catherine," said Michael. "I've enough, just enough."

"Are we there yet?" asked Sean, raising his head from where it had lain in her lap, their words having disturbed him.

"Not yet, Sean," Mary Catherine said, smoothing his rumpled curls. "But soon."

The horizon glowed pink as the train ground to a stop. They were to leave the railroad and cross the Delaware River to Easton on a barge. Mary Catherine hoped the rosy dawn boded a fair day. Standing at the rail of the barge as it slid across the water, she watched the sun peek over the rim of the world. All about her shone in the bright light as the sun swelled with the rising. Rarely had Mary Catherine seen such a glorious beginning to the day, and she anticipated a brighter life among the hills across the river.

After debarking from the barge, they walked to the railroad

BRIDGET   Johnson

yard to board yet another train, dirtier and with less seating. Mary Catherine had thought it not possible for traveling conditions to worsen, but they had. Alternately she sat on their trunk or stood, holding Sean on her lap or carrying him on her hip. So little space remained that Mary Catherine, loathe to setting the boy on his feet, feared his getting trampled in the aisle.

Michael often left his family and idled outside with some of the other men on the dangerous ledge between the cars.

The sun glistened on the greenery as they passed by, with the occasional wayward breeze managing to wind its way through to her from an open window. Still her anxiety over Sean and Michael, coupled to her discomfort, disallowed much pleasure.

After the largess of nature Mary Catherine had passed, her first sight of the mining community stunned her. Gone were the trees, with only stumps to prove they had once stood there. Small creeks and rivers ran black through the gaps. Mud tracks snaked

BRIDGET

between uneven rows of cabins with board walls seamed by cracks big enough for a cat to run through. She asked herself, how would this become a better home than the city they had left? Turning to Michael, Mary Catherine wished to ask him the question. He looked away. To gain his attention might lead to a quarrel, thus she kept her misgivings to herself.

They were given a one room shack to live in, providing they welcomed the boarder assigned to them by the mining company. In spite of the crowding and lack of privacy, Mary Catherine welcomed the added monies it brought them. Michael began work in the coal mine, which she soon learned was only a small one of the Lehigh field.

Once again becoming pregnant Mary Catherine concealed it from Michael, gambling he would not guess. Her belly becoming more rounded, she noticed a worried look creep into Michael's eyes whenever he looked at her. They did not speak of

BRIDGET Johnson

it.

Then the day came that she went into labor. Michael seemed to resist every effort to take him from her side as if she might somehow disappear. Catherine Marie, born with undue speed, arrived pink and loud of lung. With her first cry Michael roared with laughter.

"I've always wanted a daughter," he said. "A son is fine, but a daughter is for a father's heart."

Mary Catherine, happy herself at the outcome, sensed that Michael's outburst spoke more of relief than joy.

The entire patch celebrated the new arrival, bringing scarce food and some spare pieces of baby clothing.

"It was so brave of your husband to stay by you," said a visitor one day.

"What do you mean by that?" said Mary Catherine.

"Haven't you heard?" asked her neighbor.

"Haven't I heard what?"

"I've said too much."

The woman had brought Mary Catherine a bowl of soup, then left her without giving her an answer. Worrying the words round in her mind all the day through, Mary Catherine was fair to bursting with her suspicions, when Michael stepped through the door that evening.

"What don't I know?" she said.

"What are you talkin' about, woman?"

"Michael, tell me the truth."

Brooding silence entered the room, the first stranger to come between them.

"The superintendent let me go."

"Why?" she asked.

"Does it matter?"

She suspected that he had lost his living by staying with her and held her tongue.

"The foreman had given me orders," Michael said. "I told him what he could do with his orders."

"Why didn't you tell me?" said Mary Catherine.

"You had your job to do and I had mine."

There was no sense in this, she understood, except in a man's eyes.

"Anyway, I've been put onto somethin' else," said Michael. "It'll mean movin'."

Spring again and to Pottsville they migrated. More beauty to travel, more meanness at the end. They were given one room of a two-room shanty to live in this time. Only a thin wall separated them from the O'Malleys who lived in the other room.

Mary Catherine couldn't help thinking back on the ship, so many in so little space.

Their quarters became ever more cramped in the next three

years as Rose and Fiona were born to them. She knew Michael loved children, but a man could only bear so much childish chatter in close proximity. He spent his evenings at the community pub, when not in the mines or stopping home for the quick meal. Mary Catherine had heard from Mrs. O'Malley and the other women about the goings on in the pub. It was said that some of the men brought strangers there to stir up Michael and the others. That worried her. But Michael usually came home from these visits bouyed up, and she had not the heart to question him.

"Mary Catherine, come sit," said Michael one evening. "I need to tell you something."

She took a seat at the table across from Michael and waited for him to speak.

"We must move again."

"But Michael, why?"

"Because I say."

BRIDGET   Johnson

"The children are but babes."

"Am I not the man of this house?" Michael said, bringing his fist crashing down on the table.

"You are. And I am the woman of the house," said Mary Catherine. "And I'll not be spoken to this way."

"The truth be told, the company dropped the wages again," Michael said with a weary sigh, staring at the floor. "If we stay, we'll starve."

Then he raised his eyes to hers and went on to explain, "I can't even make a dollar a day here as a laborer. They'll never let us get out of debt."

"Where'll we go now?" said Mary Catherine.

"I met a fella. There are new mines openin' up in a place just a few miles away," said Michael, getting up from his chair. "I can get work there as a miner, which'll mean more money."

"Mary Catherine, if there was a way to stay, I'd do it," he

said as he strode the few paces allowed from wall to wall, his words echoing off the boards. "But they've reduced the wages so much, I can't put food in our children's mouths. I won't watch them go hungry. I'll not see them starve."

The last word struck at her harder than a fist. Recovering from the blow, Mary Catherine took a step toward him.

"I'm goin' to have a baby, Michael."

Frozen in mid-step halfway across the room Michael's shoulders sagged, and his head bowed to his chest.

"We have to go," he said in a hushed tone. "With another babe it's even more urgent."

"Where are we goin'?" said Mary Catherine.

"Locust Gap."

BRIDGET

CHAPTER XVI

Locust Gap hadn't been bereft of all vegetation as the occasional maple, oak, or spruce still testified by poking it's leafy crown to the clouds. The beginnings of vines clung to fences, and the ramshackle shanty assigned to them, having no fence, posed a challenge to be sure. Undaunted, Mary Catherine envisioned a practical garden out back with vegetables and one in front, where she'd grow white and yellow daisies and wild pink roses and herbs, too.

BRIDGET   Johnson

    The houses were built so close she'd not be able to raise her voice, or she would be heard by the neighbors. But the nearness also reminded her of the villages at home. To have that feeling of community might be worth it. After all, she'd not had much privacy yet in this country. Now she and Michael would at least have a house to themselves, such as it was, and even the seclusion of their own bedroom.

    Adopting the rhythm of the patch meant washing clothes on Monday. The women met at the pump standing in back of the houses that served all the families on the street. There they took turns pumping water and gossiping, and Mary Catherine acquainted herself with the women of the patch.

    After carrying the bucket home, she poured the water into a kettle and set it over the hearth fire. When heated she poured the steaming water into the wooden washtub and scrubbed the clothes and soaped them on a washboard till convinced they were clean,

BRIDGET   Johnson

then hung them to dry on the clothesline rigged just out the back door, strung from the cabin to the outhouse.

Tuesday she ironed the stiffness out of the clothes. Wednesday she baked. And the sweet smell of bread dough permeated the patch. Thursday she mended and reshaped garments to fit from one child to another or sewed together tattered knees and frayed hems. Friday she cleaned. Doors stood open and clouds of dirt and dust swept out to blow down the street on each passing breeze as the brooms did their work on the earthen floors.

Saturday the women shopped at the Pluck-Me as they called it. For the store took the men's pay before they had it, forever keeping them in debt. On occasion Mary Catherine bought on the tick, wondering when they'd ever be able to settle up. The very day of their arrival Michael had been given a piece of paper and told to exchange it for food and anything else that they had needed. At the time she had thought it a God sent gift. It didn't

BRIDGET

take long for her to realize that Michael would see very little, if any, cash for his work.

Sunday, a day of rest from work, allowed many in the patch time to attend mass, which occurred about once a month, visit, and amuse themselves. The women chatted, the children played, and the men usually got up a game of some sort.

T'was on a Monday Mary Catherine had met Anne Marie at the pump and had since sat with her while mending. In going to Anne Marie's home each week to mend, she had met Esther. The three of them gathered over tea and mending to converse on matters of womanly concern, whilst Mary Catherine's children played just outside the door.

One Sunday on the way to mass Mary Catherine, about to introduce Michael to Jack, Anne Marie's husband, hesitated as she saw the men already shaking hands. The very next Sunday that a priest came to say mass she introduced Michael to Emil, Esther's

BRIDGET   Johnson

husband. The two couples had just entered a neighbor's house to attend mass, not having a proper church for Catholics in the patch as yet. As Michael took Emil's hand, Mary Catherine noted no expression of warmth between the men. What this meant she couldn't fathom. For she had liked Esther from the first time they had met, Esther's sunny disposition having cinched the friendship.

    In the other patches they had socialized only with their own countrymen. But Locust Gap had almost equal numbers of German immigrants, and the differences appealed to Mary Catherine, especially Esther's tasty cookies and cakes.

    One Thursday Mary Catherine felt too unwell to do her mending with her friends and crossed the road intent on telling Esther so. Torturous pain took her breath away as she stumbled along the path to Esther's house. She rapped, then collapsed on the steps.

    The door opened, and looking up, Mary Catherine said,

"Esther, I need your help. I think it's time."

"We'll get you back home, and I'll find someone to mind the children," said Esther. "Then we'll see," she finished, hauling Mary Catherine to her feet.

"I've already sent them to Anne Marie's," said Mary Catherine.

"If you can manage to get back on your own," Esther said. "I'll be there directly. I have to get a few things."

"I can manage," said Mary Catherine in a moment free of torment. "But don't be long."

Entering her home alone, it seemed strangely quiet to Mary Catherine, absent children's voices. She stopped near the table. Then taking a step toward her bedroom, pain forced her to her knees. She felt hands under her arms, raising her up.

"Can't have you doing it here in the dirt, can we?" said Esther.

"No," Mary Catherine cried out.

Together the women struggled through the curtained doorway into the bedroom, Esther's ample form and Mary Catherine's swollen one proving the impediment. Putting one knee on her bed, the next contraction brought Mary Catherine down upon the bed, rolling to her side and clutching at the bedclothes.

"I didn't have this much pain with the girls," Mary Catherine said as she drew a deep, relieving breath.

"Must be a boy then," said Esther.

The matter-of-fact comment became lost in the next spasm. When her mind cleared, Mary Catherine found that Esther had undressed her, leaving only her shift. She lay on the thin covered tick stripped of its coverlet with her shift hitched up around her waist. Then the pains came, one wave after the other, till Mary Catherine could no longer tell where one ended and the other began.

"Has it come?" she asked of the face swimming above her.

"Not yet."

Blinking her eyes, Mary Catherine's vision cleared, taking in Esther's brows now fretted together over her anxious blue eyes.

"What's wrong?" said Mary Catherine.

The shrillness of her own voice sent tremors through her body, overriding Esther's gentle murmur. With the next pain her body would not be denied, and a shriek burst from her. Her being, a thing alive beyond her control, continued to writhe without abatement till shock after shock tore at her mind as well as her flesh.

Exhausted, "Please, make it stop," Mary Catherine begged.

"Once more, just once more, dear," purred Esther.

"I'm too tired," Mary Catherine whispered back.

"I know, dear. But you've got to try one more time," said Esther. "Now push with all you've got. Take my hands and push

BRIDGET   Johnson

hard."

Mustering her dwindling strength, Mary Catherine squeezed Esther's hands and bore down, willing her mind and body to concentrate on one long straining thrust. A flow of relief spread throughout her body. It had come.

."It's a boy, right enough. Stubborn thing," Esther said, sounding tired and a bit peeved that this babe had caused her friend so much pain.

"I'm obliged to you for stayin' with me, Esther," murmured Mary Catherine. Then with gathering strength she added, "Now, let me have a look at him."

Mary Catherine wanted to assure herself that he'd weathered the struggle of birth well.

"He's just fine," said Esther. "Here, see for yourself."

Placing the child in Mary Catherine's arms, Esther kissed the infant's forehead, and said, "He's a tough little thing. I'll grant you that."

He appeared such a wee mite to Mary Catherine, smaller than the others. Placing her finger in his palm, his tiny fingers closed softly upon it.

"Please, dear Lord, let him live," was the prayer she whispered into the babe's soft, dark curls.

Esther cleaned and settled the room, then bade Mary Catherine rest while she heated some broth. Hearkening to the noises of kettle and fire stoking, Mary Catherine heard the cabin door jar back against the wall in the outer room. It had to be him.

"Michael?" she called out. "Michael are you there?"

With one stroke Michael swept aside the curtain in the bedroom doorway and strode to her side, looking down at her upon the bed, a smile brightening his face.

"So it's another son you've given me, is it?" Michael said as he knelt down beside her.

BRIDGET

"Was it a bad time?" he asked, kissing her on the forehead.

"It was fine," she lied.

BRIDGET

CHAPTER XVII

Two weeks had passed and her strength had returned as Mary Catherine recalled the events of the day of Patrick Michael's birth, that being the name she and Michael had agreed upon for the new babe. She had overheard Esther's voice raised in disapproving tone when speaking to Michael and his own short, sharp reply to her friend. The two had quarreled, but neither would tell her the matter of the contention between friend and husband.

The demands of the infant added to the care of her other

children, at first kept Mary Catherine from taking notice of Michael's increased absences from their home. The goings on at the mine took all of his attention now. Glad of the distraction she was, for now the children had claim on all of her strength.

One night after supper Michael made no move to leave. Thinking she'd have a chance to speak with him, she readied the younger children for bed. Then Mary Catherine joined Michael, sitting herself down opposite him before the hearth-fire.

"Sean, why don't you play at the table," Mary Catherine said, running her fingers through their eldest son's curls as he rested his head against her knee. "I wish to speak to your father."

"Can I go out?" Sean said, shaking his head free of her touch.

"Yes, but stay near. It's dark now."

The door shut behind the boy as she turned to Michael.

"What is it you want to say, Mary Catherine?"

"Sean and the others have been baptized," said Mary Catherine. "I'd like to have Patrick baptized."

"Is that all?" said Michael, with a jaded weariness in his voice.

"The priest is comin' from St. Michael's soon," said Mary Catherine. "Could you come with me to arrange it?"

"I can," he said and fell silent.

Sighing, Michael opened his mouth to speak, then closed it with his lips drawn in a thin, tight line. Watching and wondering what could bother him so, Mary Catherine waited for him to speak first.

"Mary Catherine…."

Each syllable seemed labored.

"Yes, Michael?"

His look produced a dread in her. His burdened effort didn't augur well for the matter. Would they have to move again?

BRIDGET   Johnson

Was that it?

"Sean is goin' to the mine with me, startin' next week," said Michael.

Mary Catherine had not been prepared for such a declaration. It took the breath out of her. She had to think.

"He's only eight," said Mary Catherine. "You can't take him yet."

"I have to," Michael said. "They're lowerin' the wages."

"Michael, we came to this land to have a better life. You can't do this."

"It's done. Others younger than him are workin'," said Michael. "You'll not fight me on this."

"But he's only a year of schoolin'."

"He can go to school in the winter when the mine's shut down," he said. "Now there's an end to it."

Scraping his chair back with violence, Michael towered

over her, his chair's falling muffled by the earthen floor. Rising, she backed away. He took another step toward her, and Mary Catherine held her ground. Would he strike her? Fear shook her. She stared at him as he moved closer. As he drew near she saw his face soften, and he reached for her. His arms enfolded her against his chest. Stiff with anger she listened to the beating of his heart.

"I'm sorry, Mary Catherine, but I have to do this," said Michael. "We need the money."

"I know," Mary Catherine said, relenting. "I just wish we could wait."

"So do I," said Michael.

They clung to each other as tears traced Mary Catherine's cheeks, tears for Sean's lost childhood.

The following week, smiling and standing proud, Sean took his lunch pail from her hand and trudged down the road to the mines at break of day, holding his father's hand. Mary Catherine

BRIDGET   Johnson

stood her post on the doorstep and marked her son's going, a little saddened and humbled by her breaker boy. He would join other boys, most older than himself, separating the slag from the coal as they sat at the top of the tall, breaker building. God protect him. She knew it to be a dangerous and back-breaking task for her young son. For the ore slipped beneath the young boys' feet as it slid down the chutes under the boards where the youngsters precariously roosted. The boys bent down carefully to remove the culm. One slip and a lad would soon be buried far down the shaft.

When Michael brought Sean home that evening, Mary Catherine, waiting sentry at the door, didn't recognize the little black boy as her son. Coated with coal dust from head to foot, he appeared to be a miniature of his father. At first she smiled to herself at the apparition. Then seeing his drawn face, with a welling of tenderness she bent to him, kissed his cheek, and removed Sean's blackened shirt.

BRIDGET

Mary Catherine led him to the wash basin in the corner, dipped a rag into the water, and started to wipe the coal dust from his face.

Michael's hand clenched her arm.

"There'll be none of that coddlin'," he said. "He'll be treated as any man now. He earns a wage. He's man enough for this house."

Looking into her son's bewildered eyes, Mary Catherine yearned to give Sean the answer for which he searched her face. But she had no answer. Facing her husband, she hoped he would give in. He released her arm, but did not speak.

Sighing, Mary Catherine put the rag in the small child hand, while tears burned her eyes. She turned away before Sean could see them fall.

"Supper will be on the table as soon as you men are ready," Mary Catherine said steadily, acknowledging the truth of the moment.

Months later the wages plummeted again. Michael read to her from the newspapers the announcement of a financial panic. Banks closed in 1857. In some communities there were runs on the banks that tried to stay open.

Each month the share grew smaller when Mary Catherine presented the scrap of paper at the company store, allowing her a portion of flour and other food stuffs. Stretching it as thin as she could and still feed her family, Mary Catherine's experience in Ireland had inured her to denying herself in order to provide enough for her children.

Michael joined other miners in meetings at the pub almost every evening. The matter of the meetings he kept from her, discussing what she didn't know. She did know she didn't like the changes in Michael after he had attended such meetings.

"The company can't treat the men this way," he'd say.

BRIDGET

"There'll be hell to pay if they keep this up."

Waiting and watching, Mary Catherine wished something would happen to stem his anger, afraid at the same time what that something might be.

A rumbling in the distance woke her one night. Expecting the patter of raindrops on the roof to follow and send her once more off to sleep, she listened. Silence. Then the sound of running feet passing the shanty quickened her. She stretched out her hand. The space beside her in the bed was empty. Where was Michael? Again she swept the bed with her hand. Dear Mother of God, where is he?

'Michael," she called softly into the dark of the room.

No answer came back to her.

Pulling a dress on over her shift, barefoot, Mary Catherine tiptoed from her bedroom and over toward the door. She lifted the latch and started to open it.

BRIDGET

"Mummy."

The sound of his boy voice startled her.

"Sean, why are you up?"

"I heard it, too."

"It was just thunder. Go to bed."

"No, it wasn't," said Sean. "What's happenin', Mummy?"

"Shush, now," said Mary Catherine. "I don't know. But we must be quiet."

"I'm comin' with you."

Mary Catherine looked down at him, his face veiled by darkness.

"All right, but be quiet. The children…."

Mother and son, his hand tight in hers, stole out into the night. Once on the road she spied a halo of brightness hovering over where the mine should be.

A figure approached them from behind one of the nearby

buildings as Mary Catherine watched the sky glow brighter. Then she saw flames reach up and lick the night sky.

"Come," Michael said, approaching her out of the shadows. "There's nothin' to see."

"Nothin' to see?" she asked.

The raging fire, now brightening the night sky, revealed to Mary Catherine Michael's mouth curved into a sneer, distorting the ragged scar that ran along his cheek. A scar gotten from shrapnel when dynamite had blown too soon. An accident in the Lehigh field. The scarring had gone far deeper she feared.

"What have you done, Michael?"

"Nothin' you need know about."

The rasp in his voice alarmed her, warning her that the subject would not be mentioned again in his hearing.

The breaker building burned that night bringing production to a standstill. Mary Catherine felt relieved, thinking Sean would

BRIDGET   Johnson

stay at home till they could rebuild.

"Sean will be goin' with me today," said Michael a few days later. "Get him up."

"But the breaker isn't runnin' yet," said Mary Catherine.

"It will be soon enough. But Sean won't be goin' to the breaker," said Michael. "He's goin' into the mine."

She didn't like the sound of that. The breaker was dangerous enough. But the mine…?

"What can a boy his age be doin' in the mine?" said Mary Catherine.

"He'll be a nipper," said Michael. "He'll be mindin' the door with the comin' and goin' of the cars."

From talking to her neighbors and her friends Mary Catherine knew if Sean wasn't alert at all times that grave misfortune could come to him. Just the week before at the pump the gossip had all been about the accident.

BRIDGET   Johnson

"Did you hear what happened to the Donovan boy?"

"Yes, and isn't it awful."

"He was crushed between the coal car and the door, they say."

"The car got him just as he opened the door, mind you."

"Should've been more careful. Should've jumped out of the way faster."

Michael would accept no further objections from her, Mary Catherine understood. Spending more time with the lads at the pub, he became increasingly distant and greeted no one in her hearing with a word even bordering on civility.

Before the sun rose Mary Catherine fixed breakfast. And while Michael and Sean ate she packed their lunch pails, then watched from the doorway as they trudged away in the dark, the boy too old now to hold onto his father's hand.

Bit by bit Mary Catherine felt her family slipping away

BRIDGET   Johnson

from her into those blessed mines.

"God, give me strength," she cried out at first sight of matins light.

BRIDGET

CHAPTER XVIII

The few green trees that Mary Catherine had seen on their arrival in the patch were gone now. Every living piece of lumber taken to the mines. Those endless tunnels swallowed men and board alike, engorging themselves. Mary Catherine brooded over the waste as she clawed through the slag on the culm hill, searching for the elusive black lumps that kept the hearth glowing.

"Catherine Marie, where are your sisters?" she said. "Mind you keep an eye out."

BRIDGET

"Fiona, Rose, where are you?" called Catherine Marie, picking her way further up the culm bank.

"Mummy, what is Christmas?" asked Patrick.

"Tis, the birthday of the Christ Child, my son."

"Was he little like me?"

"Once, a long time ago," Mary Catherine said, caressing Patrick's soft curls.

Only as precious to me as yourself, my love, came the thought to her, warming her as she bent once more to the task.

"Mama, Mama…," Rose called out, falling as she ran toward Mary Catherine, russet ringlets in disarray.

Hearing the fright in the child's voice, Mary Catherine scrambled over the slag to her.

"What's wrong, Rose? Are you hurt?"

"Mama, …she disappeared."

"Who, Rose?" said Mary Catherine, alarmed. "Who

disappeared? Where?"

"On the other side."

"Show me, my girl."

Her heart racing, Mary Catherine pulled Rose to her feet. Together they hurried up the bank, slipping and catching at the rocks, cutting their hands, steadying themselves, and plunging on.

"Celia was here," said Rose, her green eyes brimming with fear. "Then the hill swallowed her up."

"Are you sure it was here?"

"It was here, Mama. What'll we do?" said Rose, snuffling back her tears.

Catherine appeared over the crest of the culm bank, clutching Fiona by the hand.

"Catherine," Mary Catherine cried out, "get the men. A child is lost."

"You there, come help me," Mary Catherine shouted to the

BRIDGET   Johnson

other women and children also gathering bits of coal.

Then falling to her knees, Mary Catherine tore at the rocks. A crowd soon converged on the spot, and the men came with their picks and shovels. They dug and dragged slate and rock waste away, creating a small chasm in the mountain of slag. One woman on her knees moaned and keened in grief. For they all knew no hope would bring back the child. Leaving the men to finish the gruesome task, Mary Catherine gathered her children about her and, carrying the bucket of coal pieces, led her brood home.

The next day Esther brought the bad news.

"They found Celia. She's laid out on a table at the Mahoney house."

"Too many children get buried here. Too many chances for them to die," said Mary Catherine. "The place is riddled with traps. If it isn't the mines, it's the breaker, or the culm."

"Or the war," said Esther.

BRIDGET   Johnson

    Looking closer at Esther, Mary Catherine saw the fear in the woman about to lose her sons to a trap of man's making. Drawn to the flames of male passions. Moths consumed by war.

    "It's not certain yet, Esther," said Mary Catherine.

    "No, not yet," agreed Esther with a tone of faint hope.

    "Well now, Christmas will be here before you know it," Mary Catherine said. "We should be thinkin' of cheerier things."

    "As a matter of fact, my boys went over to the hills and cut a tree for the occasion," said Esther, brightening a bit.

    "A tree?" said Mary Catherine.

    "Well, yes, a fir tree," said Esther. "We deck it out with whatever ornaments are handy. Then we place a manger with the Christ Child beneath it."

    "I've not heard of that."

    "I don't have it ready yet. But when it is, I'll have you bring the children."

"I'll come," said Mary Catherine. "That I will."

One evening in the first week of December Mary Catherine heard a knock on her door. She and the children were home alone, Michael having gone to the pub as usual. Opening the door, Mary Catherine beheld a figure wrapped in a white sheet and crowned with a tall, red hat.

"Aren't you going to invite me in?" said the stranger.

"And who might you be?" Mary Catherine said to her visitor.

"St. Nicholas, of course," said the stranger in a low guttural voice. "And where are the children?"

Sweeping into the house in a grand manner, the figure strode about the room.

"Come out, children," said the specter. "St. Nicholas is in the house."

Catherine Marie arose from her bed and Sean rolled out of

his. Both of the older children appeared quite befuddled. The younger children ran to their mother and clung to her skirt, the apparition producing in them equal parts of what appeared to Mary Catherine to be awe and fear. St. Nicholas seated himself before the hearth, keeping his face well-hidden in the folds of his garment.

"Come, children," said the apparition. "Have you been good and minded your mother?"

"Oh, yes," said Fiona.

"And you, little boy?"

"Yes, sir," said Patrick, standing soldier straight, except for a quick fearful glance toward his mother.

Mary Catherine smiled reassuringly at her son, at the same time suspecting that she just might know this stranger. Something oddly familiar, she reckoned, about the visitor's stance and gruff tone.

BRIDGET   Johnson

After a few more questions St. Nicholas stood, and candies fell from his garment onto the floor, sending the children scattering after the pieces. Even Sean and Catherine Marie got down on their knees to gather up their share. In the confusion of the merriment the stranger had quietly deserted the scene, leaving them to wonder.

The following week Esther invited Mary Catherine and her children to an afternoon tea. Upon entering the house, the aroma of pine and cinnamon enveloped them all. A bulky fir tree crowded one corner of the cabin.

"Well, children, what should we do with this tree?" said Esther.

"What should we do, Mummy?" asked Fiona, dark eyes staring up at Mary Catherine.

"Oh, Fiona, I think it needs something pretty."

Ruddy curls bounced around Rose's face as she jumped up

and down.

"Can we make it pretty, Mrs. Heider?" said Rose.

"I have some colored paper on the table," said Esther. "Maybe we could cut out yellow stars."

"And blue angels?" pleaded Patrick.

"Yes, blue angels if you like," Esther agreed.

Soon the children were busy cutting as they gulped down mulled cider and cinnamon spiced buns.

"Esther, it was good of you to have us," Mary Catherine said, leaning back in her chair with a sigh.

"I just thought you and the children would enjoy a little festivity. Winter can be a long time," said Esther. "Thank God for Christmas."

"Amen to that."

A tap on the door brought Anne Marie in to join them. The three women sat before the fire, while Catherine Marie supervised the trimming of the tree.

"You know, Esther, this is the happiest I've seen my children in many a year," said Mary Catherine. "Thank you for that."

"You do know how to make a person feel good, Esther Heider," said Anne Marie.

"That's what the season's for, Annie," Esther said with an affectionate smile.

Watching the children decorate, Mary Catherine mused, this is how it should be.

BRIDGET
CHAPTER XIX

Rumors of war spread with the election of Mr. Lincoln.

Sean became a spragger, slowing the loaded coal cars by levering the wheels with a broad stick as he ran alongside the track. Every job brought its new worry to Mary Catherine. He not only had to be fleet of foot but steady on them as well. The consequences of a misstep were too terrible for her to contemplate.

After Michael and Sean left each morning, she got the others up and fed. All three girls attended school now. Sean studied at night when he could, trying to keep up. Many a time

BRIDGET

Mary Catherine would watch as his head slowly sagged then came to rest atop his books on the table. She then roused him and sent him off to his bed. With each dawn Catherine, Rose, and Fiona skipped down the road to the schoolhouse, leaving their mother to look after Patrick and the house. Sometimes when Mary Catherine gazed on the five year old she imagined what Michael must have looked like as a child, his dark hair and eyes so much an image of the man. The same loving nature she had been drawn to and married.

Where had that boy gone? Life had taken him. The hardness of it all.

After cleaning and straightening up the house, Mary Catherine began the ironing, her mind still far afield, when a hard knock on the door interrupted her pensive mood.

"There's going to be war," said Esther, who burst in upon her before Mary Catherine could reach the door.

"That's not for sure."

"Oh, it's for sure all right," said Esther. "Those politicians in Washington'll see to that."

"Maybe it'll all blow over," Mary Catherine said, not at all enthralled by the turn of their conversation.

"More like, it'll blow us over," said Esther, pacing briskly up and down the room. "And my boys'll go. They're both old enough and can't wait to join up."

So that was it. Mary Catherine put the iron back on the new coal stove Michael had gotten her.

"Esther, come sit down. Calm yourself."

"That's easy for you to say. Yours aren't old enough."

Ignoring her friend's remark, Mary Catherine motioned for her to take a chair at the table and then went to put the kettle on the hearth. She hadn't quite got used to the new stove entirely, yet.

"What is it in men that draws them to a fight, I ask you?"

BRIDGET Johnson

said Esther.

"Sometimes they have to," said Mary Catherine. "And other times…, I don't know. Part of their nature I expect."

"My two boys are determined to go. They're really not boys I know," Esther said, "but they'll always be my boys. And as the men they are, they're bound to go and I can't stop them."

Esther sat down heavily on the chair Mary Catherine had invited her to take, then she laid her head on her folded arms on the table. Reaching across the table, Mary Catherine stroked her friend's head, now noticing streaks of silver amongst the gold.

"I'm not weeping," Esther said, sitting bolt upright.

"Well, it would only be right if you were," said Mary Catherine,

"I just can't think of a way to stop them."

"I'll get your tea," Mary Catherine said, patting Esther on the shoulder as she passed her chair.

BRIDGET

"There's to be a war," Michael said after supper that evening, his voice a little too animated for Mary Catherine's taste.

All this talk of war.

"What has that to do with you?" said Mary Catherine.

"Don't worry, I'll not be goin'," Michael said, "but others will. That'll make the mine owners shorthanded. And they'll need more coal than ever. Could be, we might see a little more pay."

His dark mood of months past lifted in a way she hadn't seen in a long while.

War does strange things to people, she thought. It terrifies mothers of eligible males, but excites those self same men.

In the following months units of men were formed, and they paraded up and down the streets in more or less order, shouldering all manner of things. Mary Catherine had seen some actually practicing with brooms, while others used picks and axes, and a very few had guns.

BRIDGET					Johnson

She had been preparing lunch for the girls and Patrick, when the alarm bell at the mine started ringing. Thinking an accident had occurred she forbade her children to leave the house and ran to join the crowd that had gathered below the mine hill. Mary Catherine saw no sign of trouble, no smoke, no shaking of the ground, and there had been no rain for days. She stayed with the crowd till she could be delivered from the dreaded news.

Then men started to emerge from the mine. In the crush Mary Catherine pushed her way to Michael, when he appeared, then pulled Sean to her as he followed his father. The men added to the crowd milling about.

Mr. Williams, coming from his office alongside the breaker, climbed onto the pump housing.

"We're at war," he shouted, "as of 4:30 this morning, Friday the 12th of April, 1861. The rebel forces fired on the troops at Fort Sumpter. I say again, we are at war. And I expect every man jack of you to do his duty. They'll need coal. Not everybody has to carry a gun to be of use. Now get back to work all'a ya," Williams finished, pointing toward the mine.

The crowd stood stock-still, stunned into silence. Then Michael, shrugging his shoulders, made for the mine entrance. Sean and several men followed, plodding up the hill single file into the open maw.

Glancing about, Mary Catherine spied Esther. John and Joseph, Esther's tall blonde sons, kissed and embraced their stout mother. Brushing past Mary Catherine, Emil, his aspect one of a sleepwalker, with labored tread trailed after the other men into the mine. Shouldering their picks and shovels, his sons left the hill.

Mary Catherine went to Esther, slipped her arm around her friend's ample waist, and together they trudged down the hill to Esther's home.

Esther's sons stuffed a few of their belongings into rough-

BRIDGET   Johnson

sacks as their mother clattered and clanged about the kitchen preparing their dinner.

"You needn't be in such a hurry to leave," said their mother. "You can wait till you've eaten."

Her sons stopped their packing and stood leaning on their guns. Mary Catherine watched as Esther gave the guns a fleeting glance and as quickly looked away. Glad for herself that her family would not be torn by war and guns she hung back, standing in the shadow of the door, only an observer here.

"Sit, boys," said Esther. "Didn't I say sit?"

John and Joseph sat down at the table, obeying their mother one last time.

An uncomfortable guest, Mary Catherine stayed and tolerated the racket she was sure masked her friend's grief. For she expected Esther would have done the same for her. Esther and Emil had no other children. The hush that would fall upon this

BRIDGET

house when their sons left, Mary Catherine knew no clamor would ever drown out.

Later that day she accompanied Esther and her sons to the railway siding. Several young men in miners' blackened clothes stood lounging against a railroad shack, some masticating a chaw to one side of their mouths. Soon a train rolled up. Esther embraced her sons, and all the young men boarded the flat cars, a few not old enough yet to have used a razor. The train chugged off, smoke billowing from the stack, and blew a last mournful blast. And they were gone.

In the first weeks and months of the war many more men and boys, for even fourteen year olds lied to go, left the gap. Mr. Williams couldn't stem the rupture and bleeding of his work force. Because of the drain of manpower a third shift was added. And though Michael and the men earned more pay for working the extra hours, they were far from happy.

BRIDGET   Johnson

"I'll have to pull two shifts this week," said Michael one evening as he rolled into bed next to her. "I expect Sean will be doin' the same, soon enough."

"How long can you do this, Michael?" Mary Catherine asked.

"As long as I have to. You see, it's what the mine owners want."

"What do they want, Michael?"

"Open plenty of mines, run in debt all they can, screw down the men, lower the wages, and gouge them with the store orders."

"Where did you hear that?" said Mary Catherine.

"It's a well known fact," Michael said with a testiness that would brook no opposition. "And what's more, I'm votin' Democrat."

Politics! Men and their politics. She was almost glad she

couldn't vote. The one gang courted the rich landowners and the other those with little or nothing. Give her a party where women could vote, and there wouldn't be wars plotted for sons and husbands to die in.

"Vote whatever you please," said Mary Catherine, turning her back to her husband.

Many a night both Michael and Sean, after a few bites of supper, nodded off with their heads resting upon the table. Mary Catherine then roused them, led each to his bed, pulled off their boots, and covered their somnolent forms. On Saturday evenings Michael often went to the pub, not to be seen by Mary Catherine till Sunday morning when he fell into bed. She prodded him up, Michael protesting loudly, to go with her and the children to attend mass, sometimes threatening to tell the priest to get him there.

Mary Catherine didn't hear much about the war, except what Michael got second hand from his meetings with "the boys".

BRIDGET

From time to time Esther would share bits from her sons' letters. More men were brought into the gap and working conditions eased somewhat. Michael found more to complain about in this.

"Now their bringin' in strangers," he said. "New immigrants to push us out."

Not so long ago they had been immigrants, a notion Mary Catherine thought better of mentioning.

"I thought you said there was too much work," Mary Catherine said. "Wouldn't more men make it easy?"

"Yes, but they're usin' it as an excuse to get rid of us," said Michael.

"Now, why would they want to do that?"

"They would that's all," he said. "Now that's an end of it."

Their discussions often ended now with him slighting her with those sullen words. He wanted to hear nothing from her. Her opinion no longer mattered to him. Only "the boys'".

"Bannan better watch what he says," Michael said one night after supper as he threw a newspaper on the floor, punctuating his words with his fist upon the table.

The clattering dishes jumped.

"Girls, clear the table before your father breaks the crockery," said Mary Catherine, trying to save the crockery from destruction.

Then she turned to Michael. "And who is this Bannan?"

"He puts out 'The Miners' Journal'. And a pack of lies it is, too."

"What kind of lies?"

"Us Irish are to blame for all the troubles, accordin' to him," Michael said. "Just like back home."

"All what troubles?"

"Everywhere. But, especially in the mines."

BRIDGET

"What kind of trouble, Michael?" said Mary Catherine.

"Some of the miners had a turn out."

"What in God's name is that?"

"You needn't bring God into it."

"Michael," Mary Catherine said, her patience at an end.

"The miners refused to work."

"What good is that," said Mary Catherine. "It won't put food on the table for your children, now will it?"

"They've been cuttin' wages for years," said Michael. "Now's our chance to get some back."

"There'll be trouble of this," Mary Catherine said in dread of a new calamity in the offing.

"There's trouble enough already. But they need us now. The war is chewin' up all the men comin' in."

Michael paused, and Mary Catherine wondered what more there could be?

BRIDGET Johnson

"They sent soldiers to one of the mines," he said, looking her in the eye. "Nothin' happened. The boys stood their ground and the troops left. We won."

BRIDGET

CHAPTER XX

What had you won, Michael? Now that Mary Catherine looked back on it, nothing. Month after month had come with news of death and mayhem, shootings of superintendents in mining towns and Modocs killing Mollies and the other way around. Mine operators had hired armed guards, the Coal and Iron Police. The only quiet had come in the winter months with the shut-down. Michael had spent most of those days at meetings. Meetings for what, she hadn't wanted to know.

BRIDGET

As soon as the mines had opened in the new year the struggle had continued. Train cars carrying coal had been overturned, and mine superintendents were beaten in nearby towns. Then came conscription. Enrollers were chased out of mining towns, and militias called in. More turn outs.

Every day had brought new worries to Mary Catherine. She had seen little of her husband in those days just before the accident. When he had appeared, there was a lift in his step and a glint in his eye that had sent the shivers through her. She believed she much preferred his gloom to this strange joy. What a thing to think.

To protect Sean Mary Catherine had kept him home in the evenings, instead of following his father to the pub, on the pretext that he had not yet reached that time of manhood. Michael had not fought her on that.

A thump on the door interrupted her gloomy thoughts as

BRIDGET   Johnson

she sat at the table, and, since the children were outside playing, she got up to answer it.

"I beg your pardon, Mrs., but I come to tell you we should be gettin' to your husband soon," said a stout figure of a man standing on her doorstep, shifting from foot to foot, all the while twisting his blackened cap in his hands.

"Does anyone know what caused it, Mr. Heeley?" said Mary Catherine.

"Not for certain," he said. "Some guesses it may have been the firedamp. That would account for the explosion."

"I thought someone checked the tunnels for gas before the men went in."

"Usually," Mr. Heeley said, averting his eyes so as not to meet her gaze. "I gotta get back to the mine."

"Thank you, Mr. Heeley, for comin' and tellin' me," Mary Catherine called after him.

BRIDGET — Johnson

Flipping his cap on his head, he gave a quick bob to her and briskly walked away.

Mary Catherine mixed flour, starter, and milk together and pounded the resulting mass into submission. Kneading and punching the dough, she then let it rise, and did it all over again, finding solace in the working of it. Dividing the dough, she shaped it into loaves and placed them in the oven, one side of the coal stove. Then she sat and awaited their rebirth, the baking soothing her soul with the yeasty smell of it.

Mary Catherine had just placed the golden mounds on the table to cool when she heard a rap on the door again. So soft it had been, she nearly missed it altogether.

"Won't you come in, Mr. Heeley?" Mary Catherine said upon opening the door.

"No, Mrs., thank you kindly," said Mr. Heeley, backing down off the step.

BRIDGET   Johnson

    A cart drawn by a mule stood outside in the street. She saw shoes sticking out the end of the cart, too short to accommodate the whole of a man. Something seemed familiar about those worn shoes, although miners' shoes fairly all looked the same.

"Who's...."

Her children ran up onto the stoop as she stepped outside and clustered about her. She couldn't finish the question, for she kenned the answer.

"You needn't bother yourself, Mrs. It's himself, it is."

"Is he...?"

"He is."

Shifting feet, Mr. Heeley plowed a furrow in the dirt with the heel of his other shoe.

"Can we bring him in?" said Mr. Heeley, fiddling his cap.

In spite of the warmth of the spring day a glacial numbness took hold of her. Putting her arms around Catherine and Fiona,

BRIDGET   Johnson

Mary Catherine shepherded her children ahead of her into the cabin. The man that had been holding the mule's bridle gave a hand supporting Michael's legs, while Mr. Heeley grasped Michael under the arms. Between them the men carried the body into the house. Pointing to the bedroom, Mary Catherine stood silent as the two men carried the corpse that had once been Michael close past her and the children.

"Sorry, Mrs.," both men said, doffing their caps and hurrying to be out of the house.

She nodded her thanks, closing the door behind them.

"Come to the table, Cushlamacree," she said, calling her children to her.

Slicing the fresh bread, she poured each child a bowl of milk for dipping, then sat down with them at the table.

"It's hard I know, but it is the way of things," said Mary Catherine.

BRIDGET   Johnson

"What way, Mummy?" asked Patrick.

"Birthin', livin', dyin'. It's God's will."

"God wanted Da to dy?" asked Fiona in a shocked voice.

"No, love," Mary Catherine said, her heart aching for her children. "I'm just tryin' to explain."

Their eyes stared at her expectantly. I can't bear it, Mama, her mind screamed as she gazed into the upturned faces of her children. Feeling the welcome wetness on her face, mirrored in the faces before her, Mary Catherine put her head down and gave herself to the grief of the thing. Her children gathered about her, touching, clinging to her.

When done with the weeping, she raised her head and dried her eyes on her apron. Then taking a deep breath, Mary Catherine stood.

"Now then," she said. "I must go to your father and see to him."

"Can we help?" said Catherine Marie.

Mary Catherine could tell that the girl only offered because she thought she should.

"Thank you, no," Mary Catherine said. "I'd like to be alone with him for awhile, don't you know."

The shock of the door colliding with the wall heralded Sean's arrival in the house.

"Where is he?" demanded her son.

Mary Catherine pointed to the bedroom. Before she could speak, Sean had closed the door that Michael only recently had fashioned, barring her from the room. Sobs came to her from beyond the bedroom door, and a minute later, eyes reddened, Sean as suddenly appeared and exited the house, leaving the cabin door ajar.

"Children, you may have another slice of bread or go outside and wait till I make your father ready," Mary Catherine said. "I'll call you in then."

Her children left the shanty to sit vigil on the stoop. She then went to the hearth and removed the kettle of hot water and, taking up the wash basin, headed for the bedroom. Closing the door behind her, Mary Catherine set the basin on the stand by the bed and poured the steaming water into it. She breathed in the warm moisture for a moment, for it felt good upon her face, then placed the kettle on the floor without a sound.

To wake the dead? Is that what they said? How could anyone wake the dead? Strange thoughts to be thinking now. I must do this. I've done it before. Prepared the dead. Mary Catherine turned to the silent figure on the bed. His face transfigured somehow to the face of his youth, no care there now. This the Michael she had known come back to her for the last time.

She struggled to rid him of his coal stiffened clothes, dropping each article on the floor as it came free. Taking a clean cloth, she dipped it in the water, wrung it, and stroked his cheek, taking with each stroke a bit of the coal from his life. Pausing, Mary Catherine regarded the countenance of the man she had chosen to love. In him now she saw the callow boy. He would never grow old, nevermore careworn. Bending once again to tenderly wash his pale body, now cold, her tears spilled onto him.

Once Mary Catherine had finished her cleansing, she dressed him in his newly pressed trousers and white shirt. She then took his coffee brown wedding coat from its peg on the wall and pressed it to herself as she had once held him. Putting the coat on him, she bent over the bed, kissed him on the lips, then knelt on the floor beside him.

"I loved ye, Michael, with all my heart," whispered Mary Catherine. "Go with God now. Dear Mary, Mother of God, I give him into your care. Love him for my sake."

Getting up from the floor, her back a little stiff and her

BRIDGET

knees sore, Mary Catherine left the bedroom and opened the cabin door to find her children still waiting there on the stoop.

"Come, say good-bye to your father now, Cushlamachree."

Mary Catherine watched from the doorway her heart riven as each child kissed the cold brow of their dead father.

That evening Esther took the children to her house, while the Irish women of the patch came to keen and keep company with her through the night as they had in the ould country. Mary Catherine found great comfort in the ancient practice.

The next day the miners and other workers came to pay their respects as they were freed from their shifts. Sitting around the table and hearth, they exchanged stories of Michael.

"How do you suppose he got to be the first into the mine that day?" asked one.

"Ah, it was the boss y'know."

"Had it in for him, did he?"

"Ah, Michael was one of the boys. It was common knowledge y'know."

"He must have crossed him some way. He wouldn't do it just on suspicion."

"That one might. Better watch his step now."

Talk. Men are such talkers. She'd given them each a drop. They'd discuss to death Michael's going. Once more Mary Catherine tipped the whiskey into each man's cup, then joined the women in the bedroom.

Several times that day and the next she asked Anne Marie to sit with the mourners, while she went to Esther's house to be with her children. Holding them, soothing them, Mary Catherine crooned the old songs. All except Sean. He avoided her presence. Her only glimpse of him revealed a tense and angry face.

On Saturday the men brought in a coffin smelling of pungent pinewood. Placing his body in the box, they brought it to

BRIDGET   Johnson

rest on the table, where the visiting priest, who had come a day early for the funeral, read the prayers of the dead over him. The men then nailed down the lid, shouldered the closed coffin, and started up the hill toward the cemetery. Mary Catherine bade her children hold hands as they followed the coffin. Sean came alongside and strode ahead of her. Taking hold on one side of the coffin, he claimed his place as the man of the house.

    Before the gaping hole cut in the earth Mary Catherine stood dry-eyed. She had no tears left for this day, for they had already been shed. Sean stopped across the cut from her and stared down into it till the men draped the ropes across the gap. His eyes gripped hers in that moment, mother and son, his as dry as hers.

    The priest intoned more prayers for the dead, and Mary Catherine pulled her children close. Strangely quiet, Catherine Marie stood just in front of her, staring at the coffin and then into the yawning chasm. Rose, tears streaking her cheeks, held tightly to Fiona, who never cried where anyone could see. Mary Catherine felt Patrick leaning up against her as he hid behind her skirts, occasionally peeking around her to see what happened at graveside. Patrick seemed to her a bit confused about putting his da in the ground. They were neatly dressed and clean of face. Esther had seen to that. In that odd moment Mary Catherine felt proud of them, these children of hers.

With the prayers finished, the men lowered the coffin, and the crowd filed down the hill to her home. There the women of the patch had filled the table with victuals of all kinds, depending on whether the tastes were German or Irish. Everyone ate their fill, and Mr. Heeley played his fiddle, adding to the festivity.

When the mourners had left, Mary Catherine, quite worn, went to her bedroom with the mess still sitting on her kitchen table. It'd have to wait till Sunday morning. Sabbath or not she could do no more this night.

BRIDGET   Johnson

Laying back upon her bed, she swept the space beside her with her hand. Of course, Michael hadn't always been there even when alive. Though she knew him to be gone forever from her, Mary Catherine could still feel his presence there. She rolled on her side, facing the spot where he had lain, and pulled the patchwork coverlet to her, bunching it against her and wrapping her arms about it. A great lump of rage burned within her. With her children asleep so near she could not give way to it. Instead Mary Catherine pulled her knees up to her chest and bound herself to the blanket, burying her face in it. She sobbed, choking on the pain.

BRIDGET

CHAPTER XXI

"The men found me a job," said Sean one day in early spring. "Since my mule was killed with the others in the flood, and since Da...."

The dam had burst, flooding the mines, and Sean had escaped while other miners had not been so fortunate.

"I've been given a job as "butty" to be helper to one of the other miners," Sean explained. "In gratitude to Da, they say."

Mary Catherine weighed what her son said as he sat across

BRIDGET

the table from her.

"I won't be bringin' home as much as Da though."

"It'll do for now, Sean," said Mary Catherine. "I'll think of something."

What that might be, she had no idea.

Looking at Sean, she wondered that he could be considered a man, and him about to turn fourteen. Mary Catherine struggled with the urge to reach out and touch him. Would he welcome the caress? Perhaps not. Overcoming temptation, she removed her hand from the table and rested it in her lap.

In the days that followed, the questions about where the extra money would come from whirled through her brain, dizzying her with the thinking of them. Michael had been a miner and at the end had still not made but a dollar a day even with the war's demands. A "butty" boy would not be given anywhere near that.

She knelt by her bed before break of day each morning to

pray for an answer. After the Our Father and Hail Mary, she added her own earnest plea, "Dear Lord, show me the way."

Sean left before sunrise, and Mary Catherine, gazing intently on her other children as they ate their mush and bread, resolved that she would make a living for them somehow. They would get an education. Something she had not been given, and Michael had had little enough of. She would have to contribute toward the teacher's support for her children to be able to continue at the school. She could not fail.

That night she slept little, her stormy imaginings wearing at her mind. At one point she woke in expectation. Bleakness surrounded her. Mary Catherine waited, chilled to the bone by an incomprehensible sensation of dread. What had wakened her?

"Michael, are you there?" she whispered, knowing that he couldn't be there. After all, wasn't he dead?

"Michael," she called softly again. "I need your help. I

have to find a way to make a livin', or our children will starve."

A few weeks after Michael's death Mary Catherine had confided her plight to her friends. And they had come to her with a bit of flour, corn meal, and other food stuffs. She knew this could not continue, for they could barely feed themselves on the starvation wages.

"Mother, there's no gettin' around it," said Sean one day. "Patrick will have to work."

"He's only a little boy, Sean."

"Little he may be. But I started workin' when I was just his age."

A hint of sorrow and more than a mite of resentment tainted Sean's voice. His tone caused her to search his face for the truth of what he said. Did his words carry blame in them? In Sean's eyes Mary Catherine discerned a wall as sturdy and thick as the hedgerows of Ireland, beyond which would be no answer for her, and she said no more.

That night at supper Sean told Patrick that he would have to come with him in the morning to begin work as a breaker boy. Patrick smiled and expressed his eagerness to help put food on the table. He seemed quite proud of himself, his little boy chest puffed up at coming of age.

The next morning Sean took Patrick by the hand, leading him away to the breaker building. Mary Catherine found herself watching as if in a dream. Just so had Michael done years before with Sean. And she had not stopped it. Here she and her children were, trapped, just as the mine rats. But rats got out when in danger.

When Sean brought Patrick home the evening of his first day on the job, the smaller boy shuffled behind his brother barely able to put one foot in front of the other.

Brushing by Mary Catherine without a word, Sean went to

BRIDGET

the wash basin in the corner to rinse off the days work before sitting down to supper. Patrick looked up at her, his dark eyes almost invisible in his coal sooted face. Her heart nearly broke within her, and the urgency to do something took hold of her.

"What's this?" Mary Catherine said. "Why do you keep your hands behind you?"

Lowering his head, Patrick did not answer.

"Show me your hands, Patrick."

His boy shoulders slumped, his hands falling to his sides. Taking hold of his wrists, Mary Catherine brought his hands forward and turned them palms up.

The breath went out of her. Blood smeared coal dust covered his hands and rubbed off on hers.

"What have you done, Sean?"

"What have 'I' done?"

"Why didn't you tell me?"

"You didn't seem so concerned when I went."

"I didn't know."

"You never asked."

Staring at this remote son of hers, she had often wondered if he had held her at fault for letting Michael take him to the mines. She heard the reproach in his voice.

"Besides, it's past," he said.

"I'll find a way, Sean."

"And just what would that be, Mother?"

"I don't know yet. But Patrick will not go back there," Mary Catherine said. "I'll not have the mines swallowin' up my whole family."

Walking up behind Sean, now sitting at the table, Mary Catherine placed her hand on his shoulder. Shrugging it off, Sean stared at his plate.

"I'll have my supper now," he said.

BRIDGET   Johnson

His sisters placed the stew and bread on the table, while Mary Catherine washed Patrick's face and hands in the corner. As soon as she and Patrick sat down at the table Sean rose and left the shanty. I'll not lose any more to the mines Mary Catherine vowed in her heart, glaring fiercely at the cabin door that stood between her and her eldest son.

BRIDGET

CHAPTER XXII

Patrick did not return to the mines but instead went to school with his sisters. Schooling, Mary Catherine knew, lighted the way out of a life in the mines. That morning before setting off to Esther's for the weekly mending, she knelt and sued heaven for an answer. What have I done to be punished this way, she thought? She dared not voice such self pity aloud.

"Mary, Mother of God, I don't know what to do," Mary Catherine prayed. "Help my little ones. Help me in my

BRIDGET   Johnson

weakness."

Stumbling to her feet, she felt heavy with the burden of their future.

Mary Catherine heard a hurried rapping on her door and opened it to find Anne Marie standing there animated and smiling broadly, anything but her usual serenity.

"Mary Catherine, you should bake," said Anne Marie.

"But it's mendin' day."

Had Annie gone mad? Bake?

"Bake what?" said Mary Catherine. "When?"

"For a livin', I mean," Anne Marie said. "I've a little money put by. I'll start you off."

Skeptical, Mary Catherine felt a tremor of hope.

"I've tasted your bread and rolls, Mary Catherine," said Anne Marie. "Trust me. I know they'll sell. I'll help you take them round."

BRIDGET   Johnson

Her vision blurred for just a moment, a tear stealing down over her cheekbone.

"What are you weepin' about? I just know it'll work."

"It's not tears of sadness, Annie," said Mary Catherine, "but joy of such friends as you.

While mending at Esther's that day, Mary Catherine shared Anne Marie's idea. Esther promptly endorsed it, "Just the very thing." The three friends smiled over the socks they darned, finding delight in Mary Catherine's impending success.

Upon awakening each morning, Mary Catherine rose and mixed the glutinous mass before preparing Sean's breakfast. Then she kneaded the dough and fed her other children, while the dough rose a second time. Once they were off to school she kneaded and shaped the spongy mess into crescents and loaves, then baked them till gold crusted.

In the afternoon both Anne Marie and Esther climbed

BRIDGET   Johnson

Yellow Hill with her to sell the baked goods they carried in their baskets. That first day, much to her surprise, Mary Catherine sold all of her wares before they reached the summit. Each day she increased her store, knowing her friends would not always be able to help her. She'd have to rely on her own devices to earn a livelihood.

Aroused in the night her brow sodden with sweat Mary Catherine shivered, expecting the scene to be before her. Fingers oozing crimson droplets. Whose fingers? Oh yes, Patrick's. The nightmare. Her children clinging to her skirts, their small faces turned up, their mouths open. So many birds waiting for food, when she had none to give them. Michael's hands had pressed down on her shoulders, a weight she couldn't bear.

"Mary Catherine, what have you done with our children?"

His arms had then wrapped round her till she could not breathe. Then the dripping fingers. And she had wakened. Her heart ached so, but she could not weep. There were no tears left in her and no time for such luxuries now.

"Catherine," she addressed her eldest daughter at breakfast, "starting the end of term you'll not be goin' to school. I need you to help me."

Catherine started to speak, then looked at her mother with a flash of anger in her eyes that disappeared as quickly as it came.

"I'll stay home and help," piped Patrick.

"No, Patrick, you need more schoolin'," said Mary Catherine.

"More schoolin' than me, Mama?" Catherine Marie asked, sarcasm lingering in her tone.

"You've more schoolin' than anyone in the family, Catherine, includin' your father, Sean, and me."

"I'll help you, Mama, if Cat won't," offered Rose, wrinkling her freckled nose.

BRIDGET   Johnson

"No, Rose," said Mary Catherine, noting the impish sparkle in her daughter's emerald eyes. "I know you're just lookin' not to attend school, because the others tease you about your red hair and freckles. That's not cause enough to give up on education. Catherine's eleven now and can study at night just as Sean did."

Fiona made no offer. Instead she got up from her chair, picked up her books, and made for the door.

By the end of term Catherine had gotten over her resentment as Mary Catherine had reckoned she would. Mother and daughter rose early to bake the bread, tea rings, rolls, cakes, and cookies that their customers, pleased with the fare, requested. Watching Catherine's interest grow as money exchanged hands for goods, Mary Catherine, encouraged by her daughter's evident ambition, marked that the girl had an eye for commerce.

During that summer conscription came to Locust Gap.

"Mother, I want to join up," said Sean over the supper

table.

Startled by her son's declaration Mary Catherine stared at him, fear twisting a knot in her stomach.

"You will not," Mary Catherine said. "You're just fifteen."

"But they're sayin' we're cowards."

"Who's sayin'?"

"Those who aren't Irish or Catholic."

"Those who would say such a thing aren't worth fightin' for," said Mary Catherine.

"But I can get out of the mines," said Sean, his voice rigid with anger.

"I'll hear no more of such talk. You're too young."

"Not too young to work in the mines though."

He slammed the door shut behind him, and Mary Catherine knew he was off to the pub to be with the men, the same men that had been Michael's friends. She had never asked, it being the business of men and nothing to do with her. Not sure which would be worse, Mary Catherine fretted. His father's way, or going off to war? Which would kill him quicker?

"Where are you goin' this night, Sean?" Mary Catherine asked on another summer evening.

"Out," was his short reply.

"Sean, that'll not do. You are not your father," said Mary Catherine. "You are still my son, and I'll have a little respect."

Sean stared at her. Did she imagine it? Certain she was that his look softened, just so, when his eyes met hers.

"If you must know," said Sean. "I'm goin' to a cock fight."

"Sean, I know your father did things I never learned of," Mary Catherine said, hesitating. "But remember this, killin' isn't for amusement."

With her last words his eyes gripped hers for a moment, and he nodded in assent. But he went just the same.

Later she had heard that he hadn't gone to the cock fights after all. He had only stopped for a beer with some of his friends. And him not old enough for war or drink.

In September the rains came. A deluge of biblical proportions in Mary Catherine's estimation. She and Catherine slogged through the mud with their skirts hitched up as much as was decent. Still they arrived home caked up to their knees with the black muck, their skirt hems dripping with foul ooze.

One soggy morning after an all-night rain Mary Catherine and her eldest were about to set out on their bakery rounds, when they heard a low rumble. Peeking out the door, she expected to see a downpour. Instead there appeared a deep crater where Esther and Emil's house had stood.

"Stay with the children, Catherine," said Mary Catherine.

"Wait, I'm goin' with you," Sean said, pushing past his mother.

BRIDGET   Johnson

Mine tunnels had been flooded for days now, and Sean hadn't been able to work. Mother and son hurried up the road. In the middle of the lane stood Esther and Emil still in nightdress, except that Emil had managed to secure his trousers as their house collapsed about them. The four stared over the edge of the abyss and were horrified by what they discovered. The Heider's rooftop could be seen several feet below them.

"What made it happen?" asked Mary Catherine.

"A tunnel cave-in," answered Emil.

"Under the house?" said Mary Catherine.

"That's right," Esther said. "Thank God we got out."

"They dig them everywhere," Sean said. "Old tunnels, played out, are abandoned and houses built over them. It's all the same to the owners…and the operators as far as that goes."

"Too much rain. The dam burst again," said Emil. "The tunnels get flooded, even the old ones."

"Esther, you and Emil come home with me," said Mary Catherine. "Sean, you and Catherine will have to run the baked goods today. Come, Emil. I'll find some things of Michael's for you to wear."

"You won't find anything in my size in your house," Esther said with the beginning of a grin teasing the corners of her mouth.

Everyone laughed more heartily than warranted at Esther's sense of the ridiculous. Then large raindrops started to pelt them, and Mary Catherine hastily escorted her friends back into her house. There she put the soup on to heat, left over from supper the night before, and brewed hot tea for all.

Giving over her bed to Esther and Emil, for the next few days she shared Catherine's bed. Then a house vacated by a miner gone off to war became available, and Esther an Emil moved in. Other neighbors had provided a few clothes for the couple and some a few dishes. Scant pieces of furniture had remained when

BRIDGET											Johnson

the miner had left. Except for the gaping hole to remind them of their loss, the couple as well as the patch got back to life as they had known it. And the rains finally stopped.

When the mines shut down that winter more bad news came to Esther's house. Emil sickened with the black lung. On occasion after supper with her children in tow, Mary Catherine attended Emil in his sickbed, shooing Esther out of the room to rest and have a refreshing cup of tea.

Scenes from the pest hospital and of people dying of starvation along the roads of Ireland would flood through her mind as she sat there. A never-ending stream of death. Michael's dying, unseen by her, she only imagined and hoped it had been swift.

BRIDGET

CHAPTER XXIII

When the lavender and white blossoms of spring were given birth, Emil quietly departed the earth. The German Catholic funeral conducted with solemn dignity, a departure from the wakes and funerals of Mary Catherine's experience, brought a reverential closure to Emil's ordered life. During the funeral luncheon at Esther's house, Mary Catherine watched her friend bustle about, attending to her guests.

"Let me lend a hand," Mary Catherine said, when taking

the tea-cake Esther had handed her.

"Nonsense, I can handle it," said Esther. "Besides, it gives me something to do."

Later when everyone had gone Mary Catherine brewed a cup of tea for Esther and herself.

"Come, sit, Esther," Mary Catherine said, patting the gingham, cushioned seat on a chair near her.

"I think I'll do that," replied Esther, sighing as she sat down.

"What'll you do now?" said Mary Catherine.

"I don't know," said Esther. "The boys're gone to war. Now, Emil…."

"How long can you stay in the house?"

"I'm not sure, with no husband and no children. As long as the boss let's me."

The two women hushed in the air charged with desolation,

listening to every creak of the worn wooden floor and groan of the rose papered walls. Loath to leave her friend, for Esther seemed strangely frail in that moment, yet duty summoned Mary Catherine home to her children. She stood, went round the table, bent, and kissed her friend's graying head, bidding Esther goodnight.

Some days later a tapping on her bedroom windowpane woke Mary Catherine, and, lighting a candle, she peered into the moonless night. Esther's broad white face stared back at her.

"What's wrong, Esther?" Mary Catherine whispered, opening the window.

"Nothing's wrong," Esther said. "Come to the door. I need your help."

"Out with it," Mary Catherine said, her irritation at being summarily wakened threatening to defeat her efforts to temper her tone as she opened the cabin door. "But be quiet, the children are sleepin'."

BRIDGET   Johnson

"This is why I've come, Mary Catherine," said Esther.

Reaching back into the night, Esther pulled and prodded a female figure forward. Holding her taper shoulder high, in the dim circle of light Mary Catherine took note of the woman's dark face and turned to Esther for an explanation.

"She's escaped."

"Escaped?" said Mary Catherine.

"She was a slave," Esther said. "She's been passed on to me."

Not wanting to disturb her children, Mary Catherine took hold of the woman's dusky arm, drew her inside the house, and led her to the far side of the room. A much subdued Esther trailed after.

"Now, Esther, what have you gotten yourself into?" whispered Mary Catherine. "And please be quick before the children wake."

"With Emil gone and the boys off to war, I needed something to do that was worthwhile," said Esther. "So..., I decided to do something for the cause."

"The cause?"

"Last year Mr. Lincoln freed the slaves, but the slave owners won't let them go," Esther said. "So I'm helping to free them."

Mary Catherine glanced at Esther's shivering charge.

"And just what is it you want me to do?"

"I think I'm being watched," said Esther. "Would you take her for tonight? I'll come by tomorrow and get her, if all goes well."

Hesitant, Mary Catherine studied the woman while she considered Esther's preposterous proposal.

"Mummy."

The small voice, coming from behind her, startled Mary

Catherine. She swung round and beheld Patrick, rubbing his eyes in the flickering candle glow.

"Patrick Michael, you made my heart jump," said Mary Catherine. "Back to bed with you."

"Who's that, Mummy?"

"No one you need know about. Now off with you."

Bare feet shuffled back into the shadows as Patrick obeyed his mother.

"Come," said Mary Catherine, leading the two women to the corner where her cook-stove stood.

She lifted two boards from the ground behind the stove and revealed a sizeable cavern.

"Tis our cellar," Mary Catherine said. " Michael dug it for us to keep food, especially in the summer."

"It's good enough," said Esther. "I'll leave her with you till morning then."

Once alone with the woman Mary Catherine wondered if she understood English, for up to now she hadn't given any sign.

"You can hide down there," she said, pointing to the hole.

"Yes'um."

Mary Catherine heaved a sigh of relief, saying "Thank God."

"Amen," answered the woman.

Clapping a hand over her mouth to prevent a giggle from escaping, Mary Catherine, overcome by the absurdity of the position she had put herself in, threatened to dissolve in a laughing fit. Here she was a widow with five children, putting all in danger to help someone she didn't even know. Who would have thought it?

Then dragging a chair to the edge of the hole and laying on the ground, Mary Catherine stretched to lower it until it rested on the bottom.

"I'm sorry," Mary Catherine said, sitting upright. "I know it's not big enough to allow a body to lay down. You'll have to sleep sittin'. Just put your back to the wall," she added, glancing up at the woman.

"It'll do, Ma'am."

"Wait," Mary Catherine said, hastening to her bedroom.

On a nail on the wall hung the old, gray shawl that had traveled the ocean keeping her and Sean in comfort. Now someone else had need of its warmth. Taking it down, Mary Catherine rubbed the shawl against her cheek then carried it back to the cellar opening.

The woman scrambled down into the pit, and Mary Catherine handed her the shawl.

"Here, put this about you. And take this candle, too," she said to the woman.

As the woman took the candle the light flickered in the

dark eyes, revealing a face of indeterminate years but possibly still of child bearing age. So this is what contraband looked like.

"What is your name?" Mary Catherine said.

"Sarah," said the woman.

"Mine is Mary Catherine. Well, Sarah, I'll help you out of there in the morning, after my children have gone to school and to work. No need for too many to know your whereabouts. Good night now."

Before going to sleep that night, Mary Catherine puzzled over the dilemma Sarah and her people found themselves in. Michael had been so fearful of them. She found nothing frightening about Sarah. Instead Mary Catherine felt a kinship with the stranger. Slavery. Hadn't she and Michael been slaves, working with no money to show for it? For they had owned nothing but the clothes on their back both in Erin and in the mining patches.

BRIDGET   Johnson

In the morning, taking Patrick aside, Mary Catherine warned him, "Don't you breathe a word about what you saw last night. Some might not understand."

"Is she still here, Mummy?"

"Yes. But she'll be gone before you come home from school," said Mary Catherine. "Now not another word."

When the door closed behind the last of her children, Mary Catherine went to the boards behind the stove and removed them.

"Come up," Mary Catherine called down into the dark pit.

Standing on the chair, Sarah grabbed hold of Mary Catherine's hand and climbed up out of the cellar.

"There's hot mush and toasted bread on the table," said Mary Catherine. "The wash basin's in the corner just there should you have need of it."

Sarah availed herself of both the basin and the meal.

"I have to make my rounds. I sell baked goods to make a

livin' for my family," Mary Catherine said. "I'm a widow, don't you know."

"I'm sorry, Ma'am," said Sarah.

"Nothin' to be sorry about," Mary Catherine said. "Stay out of sight now. If you hear anyone comin', hide in my bedroom."

Mary Catherine gathered her bread baskets and opened the door. Then she felt a hand on her arm. Turning, the question in Sarah's eyes along with the hint of an embarrassed smile prompted her to ask, "What?"

"Ma'am, do you have a convenience?"

"A convenience? Oh..., you mean for necessaries?"

"Yes, Ma'am."

"I'm sorry. I clear forgot," said Mary Catherine. "There's a chamber pot in the bedroom for privacy, since you can't go out."

Sarah dropped a small curtsy. Embarrassed, Mary

Catherine held out her hand.

"I'm not a lady, Sarah. You needn't bob to me."

"You're a lady to me, Ma'am," Sarah said, smiling.

An answering smile tugged at the corners of Mary Catherine's lips, reminding her that there were still things in life that could cheer her.

"Don't forget," said Mary Catherine, "if you hear a knock on the door, hide. I'll not be too long."

Then she was out the door with her baskets on her arms.

In the afternoon Esther came by and the three women had tea, Sarah insisting that they let her serve them.

"I've never been treated so grand," said Mary Catherine.

"Nor I," said Esther. "If only my boys could see me now."

Glancing across the table at Esther, Mary Catherine giggled then laughed aloud.

"Look at us ladies would ya," she said. "Sarah, come sit

before I laugh myself silly."

Sarah joined them and poured the tea as mistress of the table.

"It's certainly good to hear you laugh again," Esther said in a serious vein.

"It feels strange to say the least," said Mary Catherine. "But I expect I'll get used to it. Now what are we to do about Sarah?"

"I've got contacts," said Esther. "But they're not ready for her yet."

"If she's here very long the other children will find out. After bein' under Michael's influence, I don't know what Sean would do."

"The men feared for their jobs," Esther said. "Even Emil worried if the slaves were freed, they'd come for his."

"Michael, too."

BRIDGET

"I don't want to cause trouble," said Sarah.

"You're no trouble, Sarah," said Esther.

"Well, I...," Mary Catherine began, glancing at Sarah.

Apprehension appeared in the dark eyes before her. Having also known such fears, fear of authorities knocking in the night, fear of starving on the road, Mary Catherine understood. Then she took Sarah's hand in hers and studied the brown hand resting in her own fair one.

"I'll not betray you," Mary Catherine said. "We'll find a way."

The hand once cold, now warmed in her own. And lifting her eyes to Sarah's, she discerned the fear lessening there.

"All right, Esther," said Mary Catherine, "but be quick about it."

BRIDGET

CHAPTER XXIV

A few days later Esther came for Sarah after nightfall while the children slept, and together they went off into the fog thickened dark. Esther had confided to Mary Catherine that Sarah would be handed over to another conductor on the underground railroad. A strange term in Mary Catherine's estimation, for running through the night from hiding place to hiding place. She wondered how many runaways were rescued in this fashion. Esther never again asked Mary Catherine to help for fear that the children might let slip their secret.

"The mine owner has sent down word that I can't live in their house anymore," said Esther one day as the two sat drinking tea at Mary Catherine's table. "They say it's because I don't have any children or a husband working in the mines. But I have my own opinion."

"And what might that be, Esther?" said Mary Catherine.

"I think someone gave me up."

"Who would do such a thing?"

"Many that don't have a job."

"You can stay here with us, Esther."

"No, I've made up my mind," said Esther. "I'm going."

"Goin' where?"

"I'm going to find my boys."

"You can't."

"You just watch me, Mary Catherine. I've got it all figured

out."

Mary Catherine mistrusted Esther's figuring out. She had no subtleness in her, she knew.

"I can join up," said Esther.

"You can't be enrolled, Esther," Mary Catherine said. "You're a woman."

At that moment the door opened, and Rose and Fiona rushed headlong into the house.

"Draft be damned," said Esther. "I'm going."

Following their sisters into the room, Patrick and Catherine also heard Esther's outburst.

"Watch your tongue in front of the children," Mary Catherine said. "You're not in the army yet."

"Where is Esther goin', Mama?" asked Patrick.

"Home. Right now," said his mother.

Esther rose and turned toward the door.

"We'll speak about this later, Esther," said Mary Catherine.

"No, Mary Catherine, we won't speak of it again," replied Esther.

Several nights later while all of her children but Sean slept, Mary Catherine heard a gentle rap on the door. She opened it to behold on her doorstep a stout form in coat of army blue.

"Yes?" she said. "What do you want of us, sir?"

"It's me."

Peering closer at the soldier before her, Mary Catherine stared as he pushed back the kepi that overshadowed his face and revealed himself to be….

"Esther!" Mary Catherine blurted, choking on the discovery.

"It's me all right," said Esther. "I'll pass, won't I?"

"Mama, who's there?" said Sean as he came up behind his mother.

Mary Catherine stood aside and the faint light from within the shanty revealed Esther's secret.

"Esther, what are you play actin' at?" said Sean.

"I'm not playing," Esther said in earnest. "I'm going to war to find my boys."

"You can't," said Sean. "You'll not get away with it."

"I'm going, Sean, just as I told your mother I would," said Esther. "I need all of you to hold your tongues and not give me away."

"I'll keep shut. And so will we all," Sean said, nodding for emphasis at his mother.

"But, still, how can you deceive the authorities?" asked Mary Catherine.

"Suppose they do find me out," said Esther. "What can they do to a woman?" "Throw you in prison," said Mary Catherine, and, embracing her friend, she added, "Don't get yourself killed or

BRIDGET   Johnson

I'll never forgive you."

Both women chuckled at her words then dissolved into tears. Snuffling her nose and wiping it with the back of her hand, Esther took the stance of a man at arms.

"Mary Catherine, I must do this."

Gazing thoughtfully at her friend, Mary Catherine knew she could never do the same, for she had responsibilities.

In the morning Mary Catherine and Catherine Marie passed Esther's soulless house on their rounds and, again, on their way to Anne Marie's. Inviting the two women in, Anne Marie steeped a hot cup of tea for each.

"Annie, Esther has gone," said Mary Catherine.

"Where's she gone to?"

"To find her boys," Mary Catherine said, careful to keep her word by not telling the method of her leaving.

"Now how'll she ever do that?" said Anne Marie. "If

you've finished makin' your rounds, I'd like to hear about it."

"There's no more to tell," said Mary Catherine. "But I could use a rest."

"Mama, may I go?"

"Yes, Catherine, you may go. And say hello to Norah's mother for me."

Catherine had decamped, closing the door behind her, before her mother could finish.

"Annie, I'm worried," said Mary Catherine. "Sean wants to join up."

"But he's just sixteen. They won't take him, will they?"

"I don't know. The war's been goin' on a long time now."

"I wish it would end," said Annie.

"Sean says they're runnin' low on men."

They sipped their tea in the mock tranquility that lay on the room, Mary Catherine's troubled thoughts giving her no peace.

BRIDGET   Johnson

"I've lost Michael. Now Esther has gone," Mary Catherine said. "Annie, I can't lose Sean. I don't think I could bear to lose my Sean."

BRIDGET

CHAPTER XXV

"Mother, I must go," said Sean.

'Twas on a raw November evening in 1864 after the children had fallen asleep that he came to her near the hearth, sat, and took her hand in his.

"Mother now is it?" said Mary Catherine pulling her hand free.

"Mama, they're sayin' Irish men are not loyal."

"We've given plenty of Ireland's sons to the slaughter."

"I know, Mama. But they say it," said Sean, "and I can't bear the hearin' of it."

Looking into the dark, blue depths of his eyes, for they darkened when he was in earnest, she knew he would go. Her heart had been grieving already for months, for what she realized she could not keep from happening. Still....

"Sean, I need you here to help with the children," she pleaded.

"Catherine's turned thirteen now," Sean said. "She can clerk at the company store or hire out to do housekeepin'. With me gone there'll be one less mouth to feed. And I'll send my soldier's pay home to help out."

"Is there nothin' I can say?" said Mary Catherine.

"Nothin', Mama."

"If you were to be killed, it would break my heart you know."

Putting his hands on her shoulders as Michael once had done, her own father's eyes gazed back at her.

"Mother." There that too familiar word again. Too final it sounded.

"What does it matter if I die below ground or on it?" Sean said. "For surely I'll be just as dead."

"Don't speak of death," Mary Catherine said, jerking away from his touch.

Then putting her hands to her head, she rose from her chair and turned away from her son and said, "I've seen far too much of death in my life. I won't have you dyin'."

Sean came to her and turned her round to face him.

"Then you must let me go," he said. "For I'm dyin' in these tombs in the ground. I need to know what life there is out there."

Clasping Sean to her breast, Mary Catherine clung to him

with a fearful foreboding that it might very well be the last time.

Sean whispered in her ear, "Don't worry, Mother. I know now that killin' isn't for amusement. Come, give us your blessin'."

A shudder coursed through her as he gave her own words back to her.

Her dreams that night were filled once more with the starving figures along the road near home. Gaunt white faces pleaded for a crust of bread, grass hanging from their mouths. The awful vision woke her, and unbidden tears flowed down her face.

"Michael, watch over our son."

Getting down on her knees beside her bed, Mary Catherine wept and prayed, and prayed and wept, her face buried in the bedclothes.

"Please, bring him back to me, dear Mother of God," she pleaded. "Bring him back."

Prostrating herself on the bed, Mary Catherine drifted off to troubled sleep. The sick and dying peopled her night. Some came from the pest houses of England, and others were of Annie's Grosse Isle.

Come Sunday Sean accompanied her to mass. Something he had not done for a long time, the going a certainty now. The army had accepted this boy not yet seventeen.

On Monday at daybreak he left, dressed in his new suit of Union blue.

Mary Catherine found herself watching the door at suppertime each day, expecting his boyish face to appear, knowing it would not. Days passed, then weeks. As the new year approached Mary Catherine wondered where he would be on his seventeenth birthday. Each night she prayed for his safe return.

In the first week of the new year Mary Catherine received his first letter to her.

Dear Mother,

BRIDGET   Johnson

We have camped for the night. Two men to a dog tent. The boys have been good to me. One corporal took me under his wing. I was put in the 48th Pennsylvania. It's full of the Irish. We get hard tack to eat they call it. Full of worms it is. The food here can't hold a candle to your cooking.

God bless you and the children.

Your Respectful Son,

Sean McNurney

Her heart near full to overflowing, she felt like dancing. Getting up, Mary Catherine paced around the table, while she traced with her finger the writing in his letter. So much the schoolboy in his hand and spelling learned in hard nights of study after long days in the mines. Feeling light with relief for the first time since he had left, she seized on the chance that he just might get through it. Going to the door, Mary Catherine opened it to the winter sun and breathed deeply of the cold crisp air. Toward her came her children slogging down the snowy patch road from school. She'd have good news for them this day.

Having found work caring for one family's children on Protestant Hill, Catherine also earned a few pennies cleaning another house in the same neighborhood. Rose and Fiona kept their little home clean and helped Mary Catherine with the cooking and baking, while Patrick culled coal from the culm banks and found bottles or tins to trade for store goods. The younger ones went with Mary Catherine now in the early morning to deliver the breads and cakes before school. Together they were surpassing her expectations, even putting the odd coin or two away in a jar she kept hidden in the cellar.

Walking on Monday to the community well, Mary Catherine noticed it to be a fine spring morning for March. One day of sun and warmth in the midst of gray and drizzling ones. Stepping light upon the path, she spied Anne Marie at the well

BRIDGET   Johnson

before her, already drawing water. How many years had it been since first she had met her there? And now here they were again. Annie still the same, or was she? Could anyone live such a hard life and remain unchanged? Mary Catherine knew the past years had surely left their mark on herself. The bit of glass she laid on her dresser each day, after righting her hair, had shown her the beginnings of wrinkles and the odd gray strand in her once raven locks.

    Sean's last letter had told her he'd be coming home for a short leave in a few days. A reprieve from the killing, thank God. Mary Catherine had wanted everything to be right for him when he came. After scrubbing the wooden floor Sean had laid as a gift to her before he went to war, she had scolded the children for dragging mud in to soil it. They in turn had protested the perfection she demanded of them in her preparation for Sean's coming. Knowing they were as excited as she, Mary Catherine had finally relented and in compensation had baked an extra tea ring just for them.

"What a good day, Annie," Mary Catherine said as she drew nigh her friend.

"Aye, that it is, Mary Catherine," said Annie.

They pumped the water till their pails brimmed.

"Let me help carry, Mary Catherine," said Annie.

Allowing the younger woman to take hold of her bucket, they swung it between them. In that moment, Mary Catherine felt the young girl within who had run the green hills of home.

Looking at Annie now, who smiled back at her, the two giggled.

"We'll go down to your place first," said Annie.

"And a fine friend you are, Annie," Mary Catherine said. "Thank you kindly."

Mary Catherine could see as they approached her home that

BRIDGET

Catherine waited outside the wooden fence and noticed the girl's discernible excitement.

"Mama, it's a letter come to the store for us."

"Is it from Sean?"

"I don't think so," said Catherine.

In a hurry to set down her bucket Mary Catherine toppled it, sloshing water about her skirt.

"Hand it to me, and we'll see who's sendin' us a letter," said Mary Catherine, looking carefully at the envelope as she took it in her hands. It appeared to be official from Washington City.

"Come inside. You too, Annie," said Mary Catherine. "I'll not be standin' in the road for all the world to see."

As they took their seats around the table Mary Catherine started opening the envelope with great care, cutting the seal with her paring knife. A note fell from the letter she unfolded, fluttering to the floor. Bending to pick it up, her fingers shook.

The note said, "Pay to the bearer."

"Dear Madam," the letter began. "I regret to inform you-."

Her vision clouded.

"Catherine, read it to me," said Mary Catherine. "I can't make out all the words."

With shaking hand, she held out the page to Catherine, whose hand also shook as she took it from her mother.

"Dear Madam, I regret to inform you –."

Catherine stopped.

"Go on – go on, Catherine," Mary Catherine said, her voice stiff with dread.

"Yes, Mummy."

Why did Catherine call her Mummy? She hadn't called her that since she was a wee lass.

"I regret to inform you that your son, Sean McNurney, died valiantly on the field of battle."

Jumping up, Catherine knocked over her chair and, sobbing, ran from the house, the letter drifting to the floor. Mary Catherine, numb, bent to the floor to retrieve the sheet of paper fluttering there, a dying wounded thing. Annie's shocked white face hovered above the edge of the table and registered somewhere in Mary Catherine's brain. She straightened up and, holding the paper in front of her, stared at the writing, thinking she could will it to say something else. That he was coming home? What? Tracing the lines with her finger tips, Mary Catherine focused her eyes on the passage, trying to make sense out of the scratchings.

"-your son, Sean McNurney-."

Yes, Sean was her son. Is. Is, her mind insisted. As long as she held onto this scrap of paper, she still held him close. If she let go. She couldn't think about that.

"- died -."

"Mary Catherine."

Who spoke? Annie? Why was she still here? Oh, yes. They had carried the water from the pump together. Could that have been this day?

"Mary Catherine, is there anything I can do for you?" said Annie.

"Do?"

Kneeling beside Mary Catherine, holding her, Annie's warm teardrops fell onto Mary Catherine's arm. Was it time for grieving, she wondered? Immersed in fathomless sorrow, Mary Catherine refused to be comforted. Her pain wouldn't wash away.

BRIDGET

CHAPTER XXVI

From March of 1865, when Sean died, to April when the country languished in interminable grief for their fallen martyr, Mary Catherine walked in the mists. Buried where he fell Mary Catherine beheld no form of him dead. Friends and neighbors held a wake for him, where instead of a coffin Sean's soldier picture stood upon the table.

The night before the memorial mass Mary Catherine dreamt she sat at the side of the other Sean away across the sea.

Must she bury him again after giving him life, she asked the wraith. The spirit gave her no answer. Sean would live again no more.

During the service she paid no heed to the faces near her, her heart feeling nothing for them, strangers all this day. Mary Catherine clung fast to her children's hands at the service, so much flesh and blood and nothing more.

With that terrible day past she returned to deadly routine relieved not to be required to feel. Her stifled sensations a sanctuary from life. Night after night she dreamt she held her son in her arms only to waken to emptiness. Mary Catherine knew her children cared for themselves and whispered to each other so as not to disturb her. It pained her that they were forced to take such care about her, but still she resisted every attempt at change.

One night Michael came and laid with her.

"Love," he said, "the children wait for you."

BRIDGET

"But, Michael, you've gone and now Sean. How can you ask me to go on?"

"Because you must. Your brother and our son are here with me, don't you know. I'll care for them now. You care for those on your side of the grave."

"Michael, would you stay awhile?" said Mary Catherine.

"I'll be here whenever you need me."

He took her by the hand, and they walked the hills of the beloved land now garlanded in golden mist.

In the morning the sorrow had left her, and she smiled in her remembrance of the dream. Nodding to her children over the steaming porridge that bubbled on the stove, she bade them take their places at the table for breakfast. Behind her she heard the collective sigh they breathed. And their lilting voices, music to her ears, she again rejoiced to hear.

Once more of a Monday Mary Catherine walked the patch

with Annie, sharing the weight of the water buckets. She again ironed on Tuesdays as before. And Thursdays she went to Annie's to share a cup of tea and mend. With her children freed from their books for the summer they went cheerfully with her to deliver loaves and other sweet breads.

After rounds one day as her girls skipped down the road to their shanty ahead of her and Patrick, Mary Catherine spied a man's figure standing in the road near her gate. Drawing closer, the bearded stranger appeared familiar to her in a way she couldn't decipher, something about the stance, the stockiness of body, or the blue of his eyes. Where had she seen him before? It must have been a long time ago, or she would have remembered. Who did she know that would be wearing a uniform of Northern blue? Her memory must be failing her. For this man looked no stranger, yet she couldn't place him.

"Annie sent me for you," said the soldier.

BRIDGET

"Is something wrong?"

"Not a bit," he said with a broad smile.

Though puzzled by the strange invitation, Mary Catherine bade him wait while she put her baskets in the house. Then together they strolled up the lane to Annie and Jack's cabin. Approaching the house, Mary Catherine noticed a small group gathered within the fence. Annie turned toward her, revealing a woman standing with her.

Mary Catherine's feet propelled her forward. Running now, she could hardly believe what she saw. She threw open the gate and flew into the woman's embrace who waited there with arms held wide to receive her.

"Esther, you've come back from the dead," said Mary Catherine.

"No. But almost," she said. "It's good to see you, too."

Both women's faces wet with tears, they embraced again.

"I've missed you, Esther, you'll never know," said Mary Catherine. "Poor Annie has had to do double work."

"So I've heard. I'm sorry I wasn't here to share your sorrow. But I'm here now," said Esther. "Not only that. I found my boys. They made it through."

For the blink of a hummingbird's eye Mary Catherine envied her friend her living sons. But only in that twinkling. After all had she not four living children as well? That would have to be enough.

"You must come and stay with us," said Mary Catherine. "Your sons can bunk on the floor."

"The boys can stay here," said Annie. "We've room enough."

After supper that evening Esther sat with Mary Catherine before her hearth, and the two of them shared poignant moments of the past far into the night.

BRIDGET   Johnson

"What'll you do now, Esther?" said Mary Catherine, while pouring their morning coffee.

"The boys will try to get work in the mines," Esther said. "Then we'll see."

"What do you mean?" said Mary Catherine.

"They've gotten sick of living underground," said Esther. "In the old country we were farmers, Emil and me."

"You might leave?" said Mary Catherine.

"When the time is right."

It had never occurred to Mary Catherine that it might be possible to leave the gap, and she hoped that Esther's prophecy would not come true for a long time, for she would sorely miss her.

In the wee hours of that second night of Esther's homecoming, when the children and Esther had fallen asleep, Mary Catherine went out on the stoop to sit in her rocking chair. She had placed the chair just outside the door on the day that Sean had left for the war. Many a night she had kept vigil, swaying back and forth, waiting for him to return to her. For the first time since Sean had gone away Mary Catherine felt a bit of peace come over her, and she began to softly hum one of the old tunes. Gazing up the dusky lane, she rocked and sang to herself. Then in the distance a form appeared. A manly vision. She smiled into the night. He came toward her, looking proud in his dark coat of army blue. Drawing nigh, he kissed her on the cheek, then his finger tips, gentle as a cherub's wings, touched her there. She looked up into his blue eyes, a warm smile greeting her own. Then he slowly walked through the gate and off up the road. Turning once, he lifted his hand and smiled. Lifting her hand in response, he vanished into the night mist.

BRIDGET

CHAPTER XXVII

"Mary Catherine, would you stay and take a cup of tea with me?" said Annie.

Esther had just left their usual mending session at Annie's to see to the new cabin she and her sons had settled into.

"I should be gettin' home to the children, Annie."

"Your children can well do without you for a few minutes," Annie said. "You may not have noticed, but they're nearly grown."

"Yes, they are. And Michael not here to see it," said Mary Catherine. "A cup of tea, is it? Yes, I think I will."

Chatting for a time over their steaming teacups, Mary Catherine minded a certain detachment in Annie's humor.

"Do you have something on your mind, Annie?"

"I do and I don't," Annie said, her fingers fiddling the apron hem that lay in her lap. "It may be silly I am."

"What is it, Annie?" Mary Catherine said. "Out with it."

"Somethin's goin' on," said Annie. "I don't know what 'tis, but I'm sure of it."

"What are you talkin' about, Annie?"

"Jack's involved in something."

"What do you mean?" Mary Catherine said, disquiet pricking at her mind.

"He's been goin' to the pub and stayin' late," said Annie. "It's not like him."

BRIDGET   Johnson

    Having been about to dismiss Annie's concern, for she did get upset on occasion over the slightest disturbance, her description of Jack's activities stiffened the forced smile on Mary Catherine's lips. Just so had Michael laughed off her fears of his evenings with the boys. She could still see his smiling face before her, and in that moment those fears returned for her friend.

    "Do you know what they do, Mary Catherine?"

    Annie's anxious face overtook the visage of her fancy.

    Taking a sip of tea, Mary Catherine chose her words with care.

    "Sure'n he's just havin' a pint with the boys."

    "He stays too long, and still he comes home sober," said Annie. "Didn't Michael once do the same?"

    A chill settled into Mary Catherine's heart.

    "Annie, what would you have me tell you?"

    Truly, Mary Catherine didn't know what to reveal that

could possibly bring peace to Annie's soul. Men will do what men will do. And poor Annie with no children to distract her.

"Do you think he's puttin' himself in danger?" said Annie.

What could Mary Catherine say to take the fear away?

"Mary Catherine?"

"Yes, Annie."

"I think I may be goin' to have a baby."

"Annie!"

"I'm afraid to say anything to Jack, you see."

"Why, in heaven's name?"

"What if nothin' comes of it?"

"And what if it does?" said Mary Catherine. "It may be just the thing."

Gazing at her uncertain friend, Mary Catherine wondered why men worried their families so.

"Tell him," Mary Catherine said. "Maybe it will make him

think twice about what he's doin'."

At mass on Sunday Annie smiled when Mary Catherine glanced her way. Good, that's settled then, thought Mary Catherine, relieved for her friend.

After mass some stayed behind, and Mary Catherine joined them. Parishioners talked of building a proper church instead of meeting in each others' homes. They already had a cemetery, for the dead would not wait for a church to be buried from. It had been many a year since she had taken her troubles to chapel. Tears sprang to her eyes at the very prospect of finally having an actual church in which to pray.

"What do you think about that?" Esther remarked as they strolled back to their homes.

"The church you mean," said Mary Catherine. "Won't that be just lovely now."

"You and the children must come to my house for dinner

this afternoon," said Esther.

"Only if I help," Mary Catherine said. "With my brood it'd be too many to feed."

"Bring some of your wonderful breads."

"And potatoes, too," said Mary Catherine.

"You Irish and your potatoes."

"It was all most of us had to eat, and we were glad to be gettin' them."

"I know," said Esther. "You've told me often enough. But you're here now."

"Things were unbearable even here at first," said Mary Catherine. "But it's right you are, times are better now."

When they gathered at Esther's later that day, except for the absence of their husbands, it seemed a little like old times. Esther's grown sons took the place of the absent men, and the children clustered about them. Watching her children's faces,

BRIDGET   Johnson

Mary Catherine saw roses of merriment glow on their cheeks with the attention lavished on them by the young men. Her heart yearned to provide what they sorely missed. She shook her head dismissing the thought. Not much chance of that.

A knock sounded on the door just as they were sitting down to sup, and Joseph, the eldest of Esther's sons, opened it to Jack and Annie, who brought apple pie and sugar cookies to the feast, the baked fruit sweetening the air. Another knock and a fair-haired stranger entered, ducking his head to avoid striking it on the lintel.

"Everyone, this is Martin, Martin Kass," Esther announced. "John asked him to dinner. He's a new man at the mines."

At the end of the war many men had traveled the hills and valleys looking for work. Most were turned away. All Mary Catherine knew of them is that they had often bought her breads, at least the veterans without womenfolk.

Holding out her hand to greet him, Martin Kass enclosed

Mary Catherine's hand gently in his own roughened one. With a quick glance into his eyes she saw in their pale blue depths that he had also felt the shock of that touch. A tremor passed through her, and Mary Catherine abruptly withdrew her hand. She gave him what she hoped was a warm but distant smile. Then she turned from him to help Esther place a redolent smoked ham, riced potatoes, and other victuals on the table.

"Bless us all here present," prayed Esther, "and those who have gone before us and the new life promised to Annie and Jack. And bless the food of which we partake."

The "amen" resounded with good cheer throughout the room.

BRIDGET

BRIDGET

CHAPTER XXVIII

The following year in late spring Annie gave birth to a baby boy.

"Would it be all right if I named him Sean?" Annie asked as she poured Mary Catherine and herself a cup of tea.

Her cup halfway between table and lip, Mary Catherine hesitated as she considered the question.

"Of course I'd be askin' you to stand as godmother, if you would?" said Annie.

Warming to the thought, a tear of something akin to gladness stole down Mary Catherine's cheek.

"I'd be that proud, Annie," she said.

Within the month after little Sean's birth, Mary Catherine stood as witness to the christening, Annie having chosen Esther's son, Joseph, as godfather. The gathering around the font, besides the priest, included Esther and John, plus Mary Catherine's children.

The priest poured holy water over the babe's brow, then with chrism oil touched the infant's skin and placed salt on the rosy bow of mouth. Mary Catherine made promises to protect this babe from the evil one and to help him grow in his faith.

Glancing at Patrick, she recalled his baptism. Before her she saw a boy now of man's estate, being all of twelve years grown. Her daughters entering upon womanhood soon, too soon, would be marrying one day. Where had her life flown to? A bird held softly had escaped when next she looked. A girl with hair the color of a blackbird ran barefoot over the green carpet spread upon the hills of a dream so long ago.

Shaking herself free of the reverie, Mary Catherine reckoned she must be getting old to be thinking of such things. I'm not ready to grow old for I've a girl's heart living within me yet. There must be more.

Annie, with Jack's proud smiling face beside her, invited everyone to tea and cake as a share in their good fortune. Mary Catherine noticed no signs of anxiety in Annie, and Jack manifested nothing but pride and joy at their unexpected gift.

"Annie, it's happy I am for you," said Mary Catherine, embracing her friend.

Eyes sparkling with delight, Annie's skin glowed with the rush of happiness.

"It wipes away all the hardship," she said. "Jack fairly

hovers over the child. He stays to home most nights now."

The statement suggested all was well with her friend, but the slightest hint of something, not the words, just the smallest note spoke of a shadow that lingered still in her friend's life.

"What now, Annie?" said Mary Catherine.

No need to explain her question. It had been so since they had met. Sisters they had become who could read each other's humors.

"I truly don't know. Some of the men have been let go from the mines. The war bein' over, Jack says the demand for coal is down."

"That's probably true enough."

"It's unsettlin' not knowin' if there'll be work," said Annie. "Especially now with the child."

Indeed, the fear of want, no work, hunger starin' a body in the face. These terrors Mary Catherine knew all to well.

BRIDGET   Johnson

"Annie, it'll all come right," said Mary Catherine.

"Jack says he may have to look for another job. He says that's what he's after next Sunday."

A question stabbed at Mary Catherine's brain again and again. Sunday? What kind of business is done of a Sunday? Suspicion came alive in Annie's emerald eyes even as Mary Catherine's gaze centered on her friend's face.

"He won't do anything foolish now that he's got a son to look out for, Annie," said Mary Catherine, her assurances sounding a sham even to her own ears.

"Come now, Annie. Everything's goin' to be all right."

Within weeks Annie confided to Mary Catherine that Jack's trips were on the increase. Where he got the money, she had no idea. He had joined some secret order, he had told her, just a friendly bunch of the boyos.

Clearly the subterfuge frightened Annie, and nothing Mary

Catherine could say would cast the fear from her. One thing Mary Catherine knew she could do, and that she would.

Waiting till he left his doorstep and had gone around the corner of the house, Mary Catherine pursued him, catching up with him in the gray dawn as he rounded the next corner headed for the railroad.

"What do you think you're about, Jack?" Mary Catherine called out, her words edged with anger.

"It's none of your concern," he said, turning to confront her, a startled look upon his face.

He didn't seem angry to be so challenged, just annoyed at the delay.

"'Tis my concern when what you do sends the terrors through Annie."

"Annie is my wife," said Jack. "I'll thank you to keep clear, Mary Catherine."

BRIDGET   Johnson

His voice had taken on a menacing timbre, a warning. Ordinarily a mild man in his manner and speech, this change in him disturbed her.

"Jack, don't do this," Mary Catherine said. "I'm sure that Michael would still be alive, if he had stayed away from them."

"Who might you be referrin' to, Mary Catherine?" Jack said derisively.

"That secret group you fellas seem to enjoy the company of, that's who."

"You know nothin'," said Jack. "They're the only ones that care about us Irish. If we don't take a hand, no one will."

"Be careful how deep you go," Mary Catherine said. "I'll not see you turnin' Annie into a widow."

Waving her off with a grunt, Jack left her standing in the road.

Well at least she had had her say. God protect Annie and

the babe, Mary Catherine prayed as she turned toward home.

Rumors sprang up of breaker fires in other patches, superintendents beaten, and unnatural floods in the mines. There had been similar stories going about Locust Gap as long as Mary Catherine could remember. However, these new tales had the ring of truth in them.

One morning the gap woke to find that railroad cars fully loaded with coal had been turned on their side during the night. Mary Catherine saw the damage herself when making her rounds. Hoping no one had been injured, she passed by heaps of hard coal that lay strewn upon the tracks. Tempted to smile at the sight, she thought what boys they be. Tossing over a few cars. Jack would be safe enough in such timid goings on.

Receiving many a suspicious glance as she sold her wares, Mary Catherine bore the glowering, hated looks from the wives of superintendents, foremen, and mine bosses. She heard whispers

BRIDGET   Johnson

from behind doors. Whispers she was intended to hear, denigrating her race. Still she went on head held high, stepping out proud.

These days Annie fairly bubbled over, enthralled by her babe, happiness tempered by an untouchable sorrow. Jack made fewer trips out of town. Still Mary Catherine observed that these wanderings of his coincided with destructive doings in nearby patches. If she surmised the connection, wouldn't someone else guess it? Every night as Mary Catherine knelt in prayer for her children she included a special prayer for Annie and little Sean. And at the end she added one for reckless Jack.

While mending one day, the three women, sipping their tea from rose-budded cups, discussed the latest schemes of the men.

"Jack's joined the union," said Annie.

"My boys say to steer clear of that," Esther said.

"Why? Jack says the union will give the men some power over their wages, which are small enough."

BRIDGET

"As long as it's peaceful," said Esther. "What do you say, Mary Catherine?"

"I'm all for the men havin' some power," Mary Catherine said. "But what will the bosses do, I ask you?"

"No one can live on what they pay," said Annie. "We'll never be out of debt."

"What you say is true," said Esther, "but will it lead to desperate measures?"

"It isn't just the pay," Annie said. "It's said the mines are dangerous. The bosses are lettin' things go."

"Enough of this talk," said Mary Catherine. "The men will do what they will do. We'll never stop them."

"How can you, Mary Catherine? Your own husband died because of God knows what," said Annie.

"It's just that. Don't you think I tried to stop him? Did you think I wanted my children fatherless?" Mary Catherine said, a

BRIDGET						Johnson

shudder at past terrors sweeping through her.

Accidents increased in the mines.

BRIDGET

CHAPTER XXIX

"Esther," said Mary Catherine, "I fear for Annie and the child."

"I thought Jack wasn't involved with those men now," said Esther. "Didn't he tell her he would quit?"

"I think he's doin' it on the quiet. I'm sure he thinks he'll not get caught. But things keep happenin' when he's gone."

"You can't do anything to change it," Esther said.

"I know," said Mary Catherine. "Still it grieve's me."

BRIDGET   Johnson

"My boys are getting up a game Sunday after mass," Esther said. "Why don't you come?"

"What kind of game, Esther?"

"Something they learned during the war. It wasn't all fighting you know. We did an awful lot of waiting, too."

"So, what's the new game?" Mary Catherine said, pressing her friend.

"Come with us Sunday and see," said Esther, gently teasing Mary Catherine.

"All right I will," said Mary Catherine, her curiosity greatly aroused.

After mass on Sunday the majority of the patch's laboring families traipsed out to a grassy field between the culm banks with their picnic baskets in hand. While the men chose up sides and decided who would take the field, the boys, too young to play with the men, devised their own game. Patrick joined those boys on that part of the patch nearer the slag hills.

Esther, Mary Catherine, and Annie, carrying Sean, spread shawls and blankets on the ground at the edge of the excitement. The girls of the patch, including Catherine, Rose, and Fiona, strolled about giggling as young girls are wont to do in the presence of young men. In preparation for the game the men tossed the ball to one another and stretched, exaggerating their performance before their audience. Responding enthusiastically, the onlookers, observing the players' antics, applauded and roared with laughter. A bottle could be seen changing hands among the men idling at the edge of the field of play.

The game appeared to Mary Catherine to be interesting enough. It seemed that the man with the stick, she found later to be called a bat, tried to hit the ball that was thrown to him. Then the other players tried to catch him as he ran from bag to bag around the diamond shaped track. Sometimes the pitcher threw the

BRIDGET   Johnson

ball so fast the batter just stood and watched it go by. On occasion, when a player disputed a move by an opposing player, or the ball came so close as to brush the batter back, harsh words sometimes led to a brief scuffle.

Mary Catherine imagined their behavior might have sunk to profanity and mayhem if women hadn't been in attendance. The games men play at, she mused. Women's pastimes at least had practical results, such as quilting and mending, while sharing neighborhood news of course. They will be boys no matter their age. Glancing over to where the younger boys played, Mary Catherine observed them imitating their elders and shook her head.

Nearby the older girls skipped rope, while the younger ones played 'ring around the rosy' heedless of the tragedy behind the rhyme.

"Ring around the rosy,

Pocket full of posies,

Ashes, ashes, all fall down."

In her youth it had ended, "achoo, achoo, all fall down." And people had died. In the barn of a hospital they had fallen never to rise again. Even now thinking of it brought the smell of death to Mary Catherine's nostrils. Shaking her head, she tried to rid herself of the stench.

"Mary Catherine, stop your daydreaming," said Esther, giving her a nudge. "I've been trying to talk to you."

"About what?'

"About a certain ballplayer looking your way. I do believe he's playing a bit harder than usual today."

"Now why would that be?" Mary Catherine said pensively.

"My but you're dull today," said Esther. "To get your attention of course."

"And who might you be meanin'?" said Mary Catherine.

"A gentleman you met quite recently," said Esther.

BRIDGET   Johnson

"Nonsense, I'm too old to be getting' into that game," Mary Catherine said.

"Not so old," said Annie.

"I've grown children don't you know. See Catherine there with that boy. I wonder who he might be," said Mary Catherine. "Well, she's all of sixteen."

I wonder who he might be indeed. Now that she'd said it, she found herself studying the lad. Just what might her daughter be up to with that boy? Catherine looked her way, blushed, and quickly parted company with the young man, rejoining the other girls. Relieved, Mary Catherine watched the girls, once more giggling harmlessly.

"All the same I tell you, Martin is showing uncommon concern in our little group," Esther said.

Feeling warmth rising up her throat to her cheeks, Mary Catherine chided herself. You're no young girl to be thrown over by the notice of a man.

"Hush now, Esther. I forbid you to speak of it," said Mary Catherine. "Let's enjoy the day and the company. Free of speculation if you please."

Esther, laughing without restraint, drew more looks from the interested player. Mary Catherine feigned delight in the younger boys' game, hoping to avoid that particular player's notice. This only pushed Esther deeper into her merriment. Mary Catherine surrendered and chuckled good-humoredly with her friend.

"Well, that's better. I haven't heard a good laugh out of you in a long while," said Esther. "In fact, I can't remember the last time."

"I admit, it does feel good."

"What's the fun, ladies?"

So intent had they been in their own amusement, they

hadn't heard Martin's approach. Confused by his scrutiny Mary Catherine gave him look for look before glancing down at her hands that fluttered restlessly in her lap.

"I've just been telling Mary Catherine that it is a treat to hear her laugh again," said Esther.

"Has it been long since you ceased to find humor in your life?" said Martin.

"I think you make fun of me, sir," Mary Catherine stated stiffly.

"Never. I would not presume to find fault with you."

"Mr. Kass, would you like to share our lunch?" asked Annie.

"I don't mind if I do, Mrs. Byrnes," Martin said. "That is, if it's all right with Mrs. McNurney?"

Mary Catherine knew she would have to capitulate or appear entirely ungracious.

"I have no objection to Mr. Kass joining us," Mary Catherine said, pretending indifference. "Please, sit yourself down."

Her words lacked their usual warmth, for Mary Catherine wanted time to think this through. As a woman with children nearly grown did she really want to go this course? Bewildered by his clear regard for her, she focused on preparing lunch.

Calling her children to her, she passed around generous slices of her bread slathered with butter, yellow as buttercups, churned from milk given by her own cow. And sandwiched between the slices Mary Catherine had placed juicy, fragrant chicken breast meat, that she had carefully hoarded from the previous night's roasting. Cups were passed filled to the brim with milk. She shared this succulent repast with their guest. Now he'd see what he'd be getting himself into, she mused, her own tongue delighting in the smooth, earthy flavor as she bit off a generous mouthful of chicken and bread.

"I'm in your debt, ladies," said Martin. "I haven't had such bounteous cooking in a long while. My landlady tries, but this is truly sumptuous."

"Martin won't say it, but he lost his wife and children while away at war," said Esther. "I don't recall…, was it scarlet fever, Martin?"

"That's what they tell me, Mrs. Heider," Martin said, getting to his feet.

A sudden empathy caught at Mary Catherine's heart, and, glancing at Martin who appeared quite discomfited at the personal turn the conversation had taken, she kept her peace.

"Thank you, again, ladies," Martin said, doffing his cap as he sauntered off to join the men for another game.

BRIDGET

CHAPTER XXX

Rumors plagued the patch. Welshmen and Irishmen had clashed in nearby communities, splitting skulls. A superintendent had been shot dead as he walked to work in a mining town not far away. In one patch company police had invaded an Irish home, killing the woman of the house and wounding two men.

In Locust Gap no one had been killed as yet except in the usual mine accidents. An occasional railroad car caught fire, blocking the tracks, or mines flooded, stopping work altogether.

BRIDGET   Johnson

The mine operators took vengeance where they could. Terrified, Annie had confided to Mary Catherine that Jack had been sent into a tunnel so small he had crawled on his belly in the muck. She feared his chances of surviving the smallest disaster would be nil. Thoughts of Michael, whose death had never been explained to her satisfaction, disturbed Mary Catherine at Annie's anxious words.

Gangs of toughs openly roamed the valleys. Coal and Iron Police knocked on doors in the dark of night, dragging men from their homes to be beaten and left in the road. A miasma of violence hung in the gap. There were moments when Mary Catherine questioned the sense of coming to this new country. So much like the old it had become. In saner intervals her dreams of bonnier times seemed just within reach, then just as quickly were snatched away. Mary Catherine explored every avenue that she and her children might employ to escape to a better place, if she could only discover the way of it.

One day while they mended at Esther's the door flew open to crash against the wall, startling the women.

"Joseph! My heart nearly failed me," said Esther. "What are you doing?"

Annie had risen to attend the screaming Sean.

"I've been let go by the superintendent, Mother," Joseph said. "They say they've got too many men."

"But they'll hire you back again," said Esther. "They always do."

"Not this time."

"What's so unusual about this time?" Mary Catherine asked.

"In years past mine owners opened as many mines as they could. Now big companies have swallowed them up. More efficient they say," Joseph said as he sat down and drew a deep breath. "Production is down they say, because demand is down."

"Won't they need to raise production before winter sets in?" said Esther.

"Yes, Mother," Joseph said. "And when they do they'll bring in new men to keep the wages down. New immigrants or freed men."

Remembering that Michael had shared the same misgivings, Mary Catherine feared for Esther and Annie. Her stomach knotted as her mind envisioned the explosive reaction of the men to any decline in their livelihood. Absentee landlords had not cared for the starving people in Erin, and absentee mine owners wouldn't care about the miners. It's all in the caring. Why couldn't the owners see that?

"It won't be just the Irish joining unions this time," Joseph said emphatically.

Shivering in spite of the midsummer heat rippling over her,

Mary Catherine strolled homeward deep in thought. Glad she was that Patrick remained too young yet to have gained acceptance among the men.

"Hello there," a masculine voice called out from behind her.

Turning, she recognized Martin's coal dusted mien.

"Are you raising your voice to me?"

"I tried calling softer, but you didn't seem to hear."

"I was thinkin'."

"Kind thoughts I hope."

"Not entirely."

"May I walk you home, Mrs. McNurney?"

"If you must, Mr. Kass."

"Do you do that to put me off?" said Martin.

"Do what?" said Mary Catherine.

"Say things like that."

"Oh -, it's nothin' to do with you," Mary Catherine said, kenning his meaning with amusement.

Since Martin's remarks revealed his lack of knowledge of Irish ways, she thought she'd better set him straight upon the path before he got any notions.

"The way I speak and act is just because I'm from a different life than your own."

He stopped in the middle of the road, and to be polite she also stopped.

"Where were you coming from to make you so lost in thought?" said Martin.

"From Esther's house," said Mary Catherine. "Joseph had just come home rantin' and ravin' about bein' let go and joinin' the union."

"So he was one of those laid off."

"Yes, and at the whim of the boss," said Mary Catherine.

"There'll be trouble come of this."

"A union doesn't necessarily spell trouble," Martin said. "The men have to organize or be trod under."

"It means trouble all right," said Mary Catherine. "Do you think the owners will take this lyin' down?"

"Actually, they've already organized to put the men down."

"I think you and I have nothin' further to discuss, Mr. Kass."

"The name's Martin. And I don't know when I've had a more interesting conversation."

Interesting was she? Incensed at his remark Mary Catherine stalked down the path to her home and, thinking she detected chuckling in her wake, refused to give him any notice.

"Men," she said under her breath. "They think enough of themselves."

BRIDGET

CHAPTER XXXI

Sunday morning Mary Catherine heard a rap on her door. Upon opening it there stood Martin hat in hand.

"May I walk you to mass, Mrs. McNurney?"

The words that leaped to her tongue were stayed as she glanced at her children. No need for her to give any importance to his suggestion. Already she heard her girls giggling and looked to see Patrick grinning. If she made too much of it, Martin might be led to expect more than she intended. This way would lead to confusion, and she felt embarrassed enough as it was.

"You may, Mr. Kass," Mary Catherine said, putting a good measure of starch in her words. "Come, children, it's time for church."

Hoping to keep everyone in order, she shooed her children out the door before her and quickly started up the path, while Martin fell into step beside her.

"I've heard talk that they're actually going to start building a church for us," Martin said.

"Yes," said Mary Catherine. "And won't that be just grand."

Thinking she had answered with a little too much enthusiasm, Mary Catherine added, "I mean, after all, the children haven't been to a proper church yet in their lives."

"Ah yes, the children," said Martin.

Separating at the door, Martin joined the men on one side

BRIDGET   Johnson

of the house, and Mary Catherine led her children to the other side, where the women and children gathered. She noticed several women sending knowing glances her way and returned their looks with a stoic gaze that held no answer in it for them.

Martin called for her and the children each Sunday. And at other times when he met her in the patch insisted on escorting her home.

"The union is calling for a strike," Martin announced one day as they strolled toward her cottage.

"And what is that?" Mary Catherine said, trying to hide her alarm at his words.

Strike or no strike, why should she worry about something that had nothing to do with her?

"A turnout."

"When is it to be?" she said.

"Sometime this fall," said Martin.

"Will anyone get hurt?" said Mary Catherine.

"That's up to the bosses."

"That's not very encouragin'," Mary Catherine said. "Will you be getting' in on it?"

"I might."

"You'd think men would have better things to do than frighten their women with such talk."

"Are you my woman then?" said Martin.

Passion rose within her, burning her cheeks. Mary Catherine turned from him to hide the blush she knew branded her flesh.

"Martin Kass, I'll hear no more of that."

"Look, Mary Catherine, I've had a lot of time to think since I got back from the war. I know I'm not young. But I'm not without dreams either. I've dreamt of a new start. I'd like you to be a part of it."

BRIDGET

At first she thought of being coy, but he deserved honesty, and playing at being demure had never been a part of her.

"I had dreams once," Mary Catherine said.

"It's still not too late for us," said Martin.

"Would you be askin' me to marry you?"

"I thought that was obvious," said Martin.

"Maybe to you, but not to me," Mary Catherine said. "A woman likes to be asked."

"Well then, I'm asking. Will you?"

"I've the children to think of," said Mary Catherine.

"Then think about them," Martin said. "They'd be better off away from here, somewhere among trees and green fields."

"Martin, I've got to have time."

"Take time, but not too long," he said. "Time won't wait on us."

His eyes were blue ice, and Mary Catherine saw the

challenge in them. He dared her to be young enough to start again with him. She tingled with excitement. If only she were alone? But there were the children. Turning away from him, Mary Catherine entered her gate and lifted her foot to the first step, exhausting duty bearing down on her. Tears welled up in her eyes as she mounted the steps to her door. I can still dream she assured herself, wiping the tears from her eyes. Lifting the latch, she glanced back up the road. He had vanished round the corner. Mary Catherine closed the door behind her and rested against it. Martin tempted her, true enough. What should she do?

Distracted, she prepared supper, a doll mechanically going through the motions. When they sat down at the table Mary Catherine roused to see her children's puzzled looks bent on her. Everything seemed ready. Why didn't they eat? No food graced the table, for she had taken her seat without bringing the potatoes and pork and beans to the board.

BRIDGET   Johnson

"Mama, what's wrong?" said Patrick.

"Nothin's wrong, Patrick, nothin' atall."

"I'll get the potatoes," said Rose.

"I'll help," added Fiona, cheerily as she hurried to lend a hand in bringing the absent food to the table.

"Thank you, girls," said Mary Catherine, noticing that Catherine watched her, a smile playing about the girl's lips.

"And what do you think you know, my girl?"

"Someone sees you to mass of a Sunday is what I think." said Catherine. "And now you don't know what you're about."

For a few moments nothing could be heard but the scrape of fork against plate.

"Can I go now?" asked Patrick.

"And where would you be goin', my boy?" said Mary Catherine.

"Nowhere," he said. "A couple of the fellas want me to

come is all."

"Come where?"

The fellas. Always the fellas. The very subterfuge raised her suspicions. Patrick could hide nothing from her, at least not till now.

"There's to be a meetin'," said Patrick.

The word struck terror in her heart.

"You'll not be goin' to any meetin', tonight or any night," Mary Catherine said.

"Mother," said Patrick, his very demeanor declaring his autonomy. "I think I'm old enough to decide that for myself."

Why do they always call you mother when they're defying you, she wondered, even though she found no malice or defiance in her son's face. Only Michael's own eyes gazed back at her. The cold snake of death writhed in her stomach.

"Patrick, I'm appealin' to you as your mother," Mary

Catherine said. "You're the only one left to carry on your father's name."

"Why is that, Mama?" asked Rose.

"Don't interrupt, Rose," said Mary Catherine, irritation creeping into her voice.

"It's a fair question, Mama," said Fiona.

"Fiona, I'm talkin' to your brother. I'll turn philosophical when I've finished," Mary Catherine said. "Now, Patrick, I've lost a husband and a son and a country. I'm not prepared to lose you, too."

Don't give me the look, she prayed as Patrick's face softened into a bit of a smile. Michael's own expression when he'd made up his mind to do that which she most feared.

"Mother, I must go," he said. "I'll be home at a reasonable hour."

With that Patrick rose from his chair, came to her, kissed

her on the cheek, and left the house. Watching him go, Mary Catherine gazed at the door long after it had separated them. Sending a prayer on his heals, she released the binding about her heart.

"Mother, why are men the only ones to carry on the name?" Rose asked as she washed the supper dishes.

"It's always been," said Mary Catherine.

"Then I'll not marry," said Fiona.

Mary Catherine tried to suppress a chuckle at Fiona's declaration but failed.

"You not marry, Fiona?" said her mother. "You'll be off to the altar before anyone, with your impetuous ways."

"I won't marry," mimicked Rose, carefully wiping each dish and placing them in their proper place upon the shelves.

"And pray, what'll you do to maintain yourself?" said Mary Catherine.

"I'll teach."

"Well, that you might. It's sure you like to boss everyone about," said Mary Catherine. "No man would like that, that's sure."

It occurred to her that her daughters had given the subject some thought. Only Catherine had refrained from speaking her mind.

"What do you say to your sisters, Catherine?" Mary Catherine said to her eldest daughter.

"They'll have to make up their own minds. As for me, I think I might marry."

"And just who might you have in mind?" said Mary Catherine alarmed at the answer to her innocent question.

"No one, yet," Catherine said, laughing. "I'll not be marryin' a miner and washin' blackened stiff clothes and scrapin' out a livin' the best I can."

Silence followed her impassioned pronouncement.

"I'm sorry. I didn't mean...."

"I know what you meant," said Mary Catherine.

She encountered her daughters' white faces as they stared at her.

"I'd not wish this life on you," Mary Catherine said. "I did what I had to do..., so you could do as you wish."

Oddly she felt no recrimination at her daughter's words. Instead peace swelled within her hopeful breast, certain now that her daughters would strive not to repeat the hardships of the past. But Patrick, what about Patrick?

BRIDGET

CHAPTER XXXII

Patrick's canvas trousers lay on her lap, and Mary Catherine's fingers, toying with the rough material, forgot to mend.

"Mary Catherine, where are you?" said Esther. "I've been speaking to you for five minutes and you haven't heard a thing I've said."

Shaken free of her musing Mary Catherine gazed at her friend.

"All Patrick and Martin have been talkin' about lately,

Esther, is the unions. Why do men set such store by them?"

"My boys, too," Esther said.

"I don't like it, atall, atall."

Fear crept into the room on tiptoe, pulling a shade over the bright day without, a fourth partner in the sewing circle, dampening chatter of gayer times.

"My Jack's been goin' again of an evenin'," said Annie.

"What can we do?" said Mary Catherine.

"Leave," Esther said.

"I can't leave," said Annie. "Jack'll not go."

"And go where, Esther?" asked Mary Catherine.

"West," she replied. "My boys want to buy a farm."

"You'd leave me, Mary Catherine?" said Annie.

"I've not said anything about leavin'," said Mary Catherine.

"Well, if you must, you must," Annie said, sighing softly.

BRIDGET   Johnson

"Annie, I've no reason to leave. I'm makin' a livin' with my bakin' right here. And I've no money for buyin' land," said Mary Catherine. "And if I did, I wouldn't trust it. My family were thrown off the land. It's never really yours, is it?"

"We can't just wait, hoping nothing'll happen," said Esther.

"Please, can we talk of somethin' else," Annie said. "I'll not go without Jack and he won't go."

"Yes, Esther, let's quit this talk," said Mary Catherine, resolving to rid herself and her friends of their fearful intruder. "What about that new twist in your bread pudding, Esther?"

"Just so you'd believe me, I made some for us to try," said Esther.

Bustling about, Esther brought three bowls to the table, cinnamon and chocolate scenting the air.

"Umm…," murmured Mary Catherine, inhaling the sweetness, "you've cut chunks of chocolate into it, instead of usin' raisins."

"Here, Mary Catherine, try this sweetened cream on it," said Annie, handing the cream pitcher to her. "Esther, it fairly melts in the mouth."

Mary Catherine tipped the pitcher and watched the silken rivulet caress the dessert. Then taking a spoonful into her mouth, she savored its richness.

"I don't know if you're saint or sinner, Esther, but temptress you surely are," Mary Catherine said.

"It's heaven it is, Esther, and no denyin' it," said Annie.

"Not quite, Annie," Esther said. "But it'll do for now."

Strolling home late that afternoon lost in a reverie produced by the unexpected but pleasurable delicacy, Mary Catherine failed to hear the voice at first. Not altogether unwelcome, still it extinguished her fancies in an instant.

"Mary Catherine, I'd be pleased if you would let me speak

BRIDGET   Johnson

to you."

"It's a free world, Martin Kass."

Such formal talk from Martin. What could he mean by it?

"I'd be after invitin' you in to tea, if you like?" she said.

"I would like a cup. If you'd be so kind," he replied.

Puzzled, Mary Catherine glanced at him. He'd cleaned up. And removing his hat, Martin followed her into the house.

"Have a seat, Martin," said Mary Catherine. "I'll get the tea ready directly."

A prick of apprehension tickled its way up the back of her neck. What was he up to? Was he going away? And what if he did. What was that to her?

"Mary Catherine, would you please sit down?" said Martin. "It's hard to talk to you while you prance about as if you're dancing on hot coals."

"I'm not prancin', I'll have you know."

"I'm sorry. I don't know how to talk to you."

"I'd be pleased if you'd quit beatin' about the bush and say what you've come to say," said Mary Catherine.

Martin caught her hand as she passed near him and gently pulled her close.

"Please, sit down and hear me out."

Holding her hand betwixt his own, Martin caressed it tenderly. Mary Catherine sat down at the table and, unable to resist the impulse, raised her eyes to his. Those unflinching blue eyes of his questioned her very soul.

"… land out west."

What had he said? He's going far away just as she'd feared.

"Veterans are being given first choice," Martin went on. "A hundred and sixty acres. Rich farm land I'm told."

What had this to do with her? If only he'd stop talking of

BRIDGET   Johnson

the land.

"Did you hear me, Mary Catherine?" Martin said.

What had she heard? Him yammering on and on about some land.

"You're goin' away and something about land," said Mary Catherine.

"Yes, I'm going away," said Martin. "But, I want you to come with me."

Knocking over her chair as she rose, Mary Catherine wrenched her hand from his.

"I can't just up and be off, now can I?"

"Calm yourself."

"Calm is it?" said Mary Catherine. "You come here talkin' about leavin' and land and you want…. Just what is it you want from me?"

"I want you to be my wife," Martin said. "We'll start a new

life on the land."

Unnerved by Martin's bold proposal Mary Catherine distractedly grasped the fallen chair, set it upright, and collapsed upon the seat.

"We'll be married, and you and the children will come with me."

Momentarily confused she didn't know how to answer him. Green fields and wild flowers danced through her brain. Then Mary Catherine remembered. He had said he would buy land.

"We'll have a farm," Martin said. "A fit place to raise children."

A farm? She felt weak.

"What's the matter?" said Martin.

"I can't," Mary Catherine said.

"You can't what?" said Martin. "Tell me."

"You don't understand," Mary Catherine said.

BRIDGET Johnson

The shrillness of her voice grated on her ears. Cold, so cold she felt.

"What don't I understand?"

His voice came to her from such a distance. A tear trickled down her cheek, and Mary Catherine tasted the salt of it in her mouth.

"In Ireland we lived on a farm, me and my family. We couldn't own the land, not even the house we lived in. Then the potatoes died. Year after year the crops failed. It's what we lived on. The landlord sent us bread at first and a little tea. Then it stopped. Da couldn't pay the rent. One day the sheriff and his men came. They told us to leave the house. My father refused. He stood his ground, he did, and faced them down. I stood beside him that day."

"One of the men made a grab for him, and he brushed him off. The next thing, one of them had a club. I heard it hit himself.

BRIDGET   Johnson

I can't tell you what it sounded like. But I'll never forget it. Da dropped like a gored ox, his face all bloodied. Then two of them dragged him out, and I saw them put their boot to him. They kicked him into the ditch."

"My mother stood on the step to the house, the children hangin' onto her skirt weepin', while she looked on him and his shame. When I scrambled down to him, I found he was still alive. I tried to pull him up, but I hadn't the strength. One of our tormentors reached out a hand to us. He was grinnin' when I looked up at him. Just sport to him I shouldn't be surprised. Well I wanted none of that, so I knocked his hand away. And I gave him such a look he backed off. With my mother helpin', we got himself sittin' up again on the side of the road."

"With us still lookin' on, I saw a man with a torch touch it to our roof. I don't remember much about goin' into the burnin' house. But I remember standin' in front of my mother, a loaf of

BRIDGET

bread in one hand and a candlestick in the other. My mother was lookin' at me, a queer smile on her face. I remember thinkin' that odd. She must have thought I'd gone round the bend. That was the last time I ever saw her smile. Not even on my weddin' day."

"What happened then?" said Martin. "Where did you stay?"

"That night we hung onto each other by the side of the road. It rained just to add to our misery. The rain, of course, put an end to any fire to keep off the chill. We scavenged through the ruins and found a kettle and some metal smalls that survived the fire. We kept them to trade for food. My brother, Sean, died because of that night."

Weary with the telling, she laid her head on her folded arms on the table before her. His hand gently rubbed her back, and she rested in the comfort of his touch..

"So, now you see," she said.

"Yes, I see," said Martin.

"A farm to me means a life akin to slavery," said Mary Catherine.

"But, we'll own the land," Martin said.

Own? Such a simple word. Her experience couldn't grasp it.

"Own?" said Mary Catherine looking up at him. "Does anyone ever own the land?"

"Yes. It will be ours," Martin said. "Trust me."

BRIDGET

CHAPTER XXXIII

Trust me, he had said. In bed that night Mary Catherine stared at a ceiling she could not see. Oh Michael, what should I do? When finally she did sleep, ghosts from the past inhabited her dreams. First came the Seans, all smiles. The brother she loved bade her not forget him, nor the land from which she sprang. Her son appeared as he had in the vision, so real, yet ……… Father and mother revealed themselves hand in hand and whispered, "Be happy, Cushlamacree." Then Michael's face came close to her own, so close she saw the tears in his coal black eyes.

"You're mine. Don't you forget that."

"Please let me go, Michael."

Her wrist in his grasp, she couldn't pull free no matter how she struggled.

"Let me go, Michael," she cried. "In the name of God let me go."

Invoking the name of God loosened his hold, and Mary Catherine slept in peace the balance of the night.

"Mother, I'll be off now," Patrick announced at breakfast. "Don't wait supper, for I'll be home late."

Mary Catherine hadn't the fortitude to fight him, but still she must protest.

"What'll you be up to, Patrick?"

"Nothin' you need worry yourself about," he said, getting up from the table. "Some things are best not known."

BRIDGET   Johnson

"Patrick, you're the man of the house now," said Mary Catherine, standing to face her son. "You've obligations."

"I know, Mother," said Patrick. "But there are things I must do."

As he shut the door between them her arms hung useless, helpless she was to hold him close and keep him safe.

With the mixing of the ingredients for her breads, Mary Catherine felt her strength return, and she gave the dough what for with vigor. After filling the baskets with her sweet-smelling rolls and breads, Mary Catherine's daughters carried them to her customers before they went to school. She'd collect the money due at the end of the week.

Still feeling low, she expected she'd need her friends this sewing day, welcoming the chore that brought the three close each week. She wondered if they ever felt the need of her company in quite the same way.

"Put your mind at rest on that," said Esther, binding away the edge of a quilt with sure, quick movements.

"When Emil took sick, I don't know what I'd have done without you two."

"I wish I knew what Patrick's into," said Mary Catherine. "I suspect he's goin' off with the men to do mischief."

"How old is he?" said Annie.

"Just fifteen," Mary Catherine said. "But thinks himself a man he does."

"He's not old enough to get accepted, Mary Catherine," said Annie.

"I'm not sure that'd put'em off."

Her desperate words hung in the air between them.

"Get him away from here," said Esther.

"And just how do I do that?" said Mary Catherine.

"Seems you've had an offer."

BRIDGET   Johnson

"And what offer might you be referrin' to?" Mary Catherine said testily.

"Yes, what offer's been made to you?" Annie asked.

"No one's business but my own, Annie, to be sure."

"Smooth your feathers, Mary Catherine," Esther said. "I'm only thinking of you and the children."

"Mary Catherine, have you been holdin' out on us?" said Annie.

A coy smile played about Annie's lips when Mary Catherine turned a quick look in her direction.

"How has Jack been?" Mary Catherine said.

"Changin' the subject are you?" said Annie.

"Yes, if you must know," said Mary Catherine. "I think we've discussed me enough for one day."

"You two aren't the only ones worried about the men folk," Esther said. "Ever since my boys got home from the war they've been involved in something they won't talk about. I don't know what. Something to do with the low wages they're making. They've had no work for weeks at a time."

"Won't the owners ever understand that the men can only be pushed so far?" said Annie.

"The owners aren't concerned," Mary Catherine said. "Nobody bothers them with the troubles of the likes of us."

"We can't just sit here and watch it happen," said Esther. "I didn't go to war and bring my boys home for this."

Mary Catherine had quit mending altogether, and she glanced at her friends whose hands had also slackened in their stitching.

"Emil and me were farmers before we came here," Esther said. "My boys belong on the land, not under it. I think I'll ask them again about farming."

"Annie, what'll you do?" said Mary Catherine.

BRIDGET — Johnson

"What'll I do," said Annie. "I'll stay by my husband's side, to be sure."

"I think we need more tea," Esther said, rising from her chair and shaking her head.

"I'll miss you, Mary Catherine," said Annie.

"What makes you think I'm goin'?" Mary Catherine said. "Nothin's been decided."

Annie's head lowered so that Mary Catherine could not see her eyes.

"But you should go, if you can."

"And marry a man I don't fancy?" said Mary Catherine.

Annie raised her head and their eyes met.

"We can afford love when we're young," Annie said.

"Enough of this talk now," said Esther, placing the teapot and pie pan on the table. "Taste this pie. You'd have to go a far piece to find better. I put raisins in with the apples and nutmeg and cinnamon, of course."

Sitting before the hearth fire that evening, Mary Catherine fretted over her children's future, studying them each in turn. As her gaze fell on Patrick, he rose, crossed to the door, and, grasping the latch, turned to look at her.

"Patrick,...?" she started to say.

"Yes, Mother."

"Nothin," Mary Catherine said, "nothin' atall."

Walking back to the hearth, Patrick bent toward his mother and kissed her gently on her brow. Then he left Mary Catherine gazing after him, the door closing behind him. Just so had Sean done before he went off to die.

Turning to the fire, Mary Catherine stared into the blood-red, burning coals before her and decided.

BRIDGET

CHAPTER XXXIV

Mary Catherine leaned on her gate, watching the men slouch along the patch road toward home, clothes no longer stiffened with coal dust and dirt. A washing up building had been added to the patch near the mines, where they changed and left their garb till the week was out.

Distracted by her musings Mary Catherine only noticed him when he hailed her, his towhead bobbing above the other miners. Having caught her attention, Martin smiled at her. In turn she smiled back, opening the gate and waving to him.

"Martin, I would have a word with you," said Mary Catherine as he came near. "Would you take a cup of tea with me?"

He reached for her hand where it rested on top of the gate. Mary Catherine drew back, avoiding his touch, thus hoping to curb his enthusiasm, for she had serious matters to discuss. She mounted the steps and crossed the threshold before him.

"Would you take a seat at the table, please, Martin," Mary Catherine said.

Flustered in the formality of the moment Mary Catherine busied herself with the teapot and sliced a tea-ring. Rattling cup and saucer, she first steadied herself, then placed the tea and cake before him.

"Mary Catherine, won't you please sit down," said Martin. "Your constant motion is making me dizzy."

She walked round the table taking a seat opposite him.

"Martin, I have decided to accept your offer," Mary Catherine said.

"You have?" he said.

"Yes, I have."

"Fine."

"Is that all you can say?" said Mary Catherine.

"What more is there to say?" said Martin.

His even tone she could tell cost him considerable effort. Knowing that, her own tension eased.

"We're friends and…."

"You needn't explain," Martin said.

"I'll be a good wife."

"I know you will."

"I'm sorry, but I have to get the children away from here," said Mary Catherine, bowing her head till it rested upon her arms.

BRIDGET

Sobbing her desperation, Mary Catherine felt strong hands pulling her up and went willingly into Martin's arms. She ached to be held and rested her head on his chest. Mary Catherine had forgotten how it felt to be caressed and cared for, even before Michael had died. Cupping her face with his rough but gentle hands, Martin kissed her full on the mouth. For an instant something deep within her sprang to life, a stirring of the dead. Drawing back from his embrace, Mary Catherine stared at the cracks in the floor, not daring to look into his eyes. Such foolishness. She could hardly be taken for an innocent at her age. Get over it quick, woman, or he might think better of his bargain, Mary Catherine chided herself.

"I'll speak to the priest," said Martin. "We just might marry in the new church."

"Is it to be finished soon?" she asked.

"In a bit of a hurry are we?"

Provoked by his flippancy, Mary Catherine retorted, "Not atall. I can wait."

"Have I offended you?"

She remained silent, refusing to foster any delusions in him touching on their coupling.

"How much time might you need to be ready?" he said.

"I'll be ready when you are," said Mary Catherine.

"Come now, Mary Catherine," Martin said, taking her hands in his.

He peered into her face, a smile curving his lips. Concern for her was all she discerned in his clear blue eyes. Not willing to smother it, a giggle escaped her lips.

"We'll leave it to the priest then," Martin said, letting go of her hands.

Fiona and Rose burst through the door bringing further conversation to a halt. Frowning at her daughters, Mary Catherine brushed aside their questioning looks, while Martin's very presence in the house subdued them.

"I'll leave now and let you explain," said Martin, "while I see to the arrangements."

The door had but closed when the inquisition began.

"Explain what, Mama?" asked Rose.

"Arrangements for what?" added Fiona with a note of suspicion in her voice.

"Martin and I are goin' to marry," said Mary Catherine.

"How can you, Mother," cried Fiona.

"Where will we live?" Rose asked.

Then Catherine entered the house, and Mary Catherine smiled at her eldest, hoping to win her to her side.

"What's all the clatterin' about," said Catherine. "You two hush and let Mother speak."

"Martin is offerin' to take us all away from here," Mary

BRIDGET   Johnson

Catherine said. "Away from the coal dust and maimin' and death."

"Mother, where will we be goin'?" said Catherine.

"To where you can walk in green fields by sweet smellin' streams. The kind I knew as a girl."

"And just where would that be?" said a brusque male voice from the shadows near the door.

"Patrick, I want us to go away from here," Mary Catherine said, swinging round to answer her son's curt query. "I want you out of danger."

"What danger would that be?" said Patrick.

"The same as killed your father."

"What if I won't go?" said Patrick.

"I can't force you to come with us," Mary Catherine said. "You know that all too well. But, Patrick, think. What would your father want for you? Ask yourself that?"

"He'd want me to stick with the boyos."

"Would he really?" said Mary Catherine. "Wasn't he always fightin' for a better chance for us all?"

"What would he say to your marryin' an outsider?" said her son with asperity.

Anger and fear of the possible loss of her son fought a fierce battle within her.

"We best say no more on the subject tonight," Mary Catherine said staunchly, "or we'll be sayin' somethin' we'll regret."

Patrick turned from her, and the shock of wood hitting wood shook the place as he slammed out of the house. Stretching out her hand toward his departing back, Mary Catherine wished she knew the charm that would draw him back to her. In her heart she prayed, then she turned to her daughters, her hand falling uselessly to her side.

"Well, what of you?" Mary Catherine said. "Are you of the

same mind as your brother?"

"We'll come, Mother," said Catherine.

Mary Catherine turned to face Fiona and Rose, and they nodded their assent.

"That's settled then," she said.

That night in her dreams Patrick fell, and, reaching for him, she couldn't catch him back. Waking, Mary Catherine felt a chill within her breast.

"Michael, please help me. Give me the words," she pleaded. "You were always good with the words. Give me the words to change his heart."

BRIDGET

CHAPTER XXXV

"Do you want me to speak to him, Mary Catherine?" said Martin.

"No, Martin, I'll talk to him."

"Maybe we should just hogtie him and toss him into one of the coal cars."

Shocked at what Martin had said, Mary Catherine looked to see a smile lifting the corners of his mouth.

"Are you playin' with me, Martin Kass?" Mary Catherine

said.

He chuckled, and she laughed at his amusement.

"I'll make an Irishman of you yet. You've already got the knack of turnin' a tragedy into a laughin' matter."

"Seriously, would you like me to have a word with Patrick?" said Martin.

"It's kind of you to offer," Mary Catherine said. "But he's my son. He'll just think you're interferin'."

For the rest of that day into the next Mary Catherine carried the stone weight of it somewhere next to her heart, mulling over what she could say to change Patrick's way of thinking. In spare moments she prayed, kneeling by her bed with her head in her hands.

Tension crowded so thick over that evening meal Mary Catherine could almost reach out and grasp it. Except for the rattling of utensil against plate silence prevailed, and she continued to worry the food about her plate. With the meal finished, her daughters cleared the table, while Patrick picked up his cap and made for the door.

"Patrick, I'd have a word with you," Mary Catherine called after him.

His back tensed.

"Please, Patrick, only a minute," she said, plying her most enticing maternal tone.

His shoulders relaxed as she waited for his answer, and, turning to her, he gave her look for look.

"The boys are waitin' on me," he said.

"I know," said Mary Catherine, sensing she must tread lightly here.

"All right," Patrick said. "But make it quick."

Mary Catherine nodded at Catherine who handed her sisters their shawls. Then the girls left mother and son alone in the house.

BRIDGET　　　　　　　　　　Johnson

They stared at each other across the short expanse of the room, a chasm to be bridged, a rent to be seamed, a bond torn asunder to be made whole.

Gathering her mother's wit about her, Mary Catherine girded herself for yet another travail to deliver this endangered child.

"I know what you're goin' to say, Mother," said Patrick. "There's nothin' to be said that can change my mind."

"I'm only askin' you to think, Patrick. Think what your Da would want."

"He'd want me to carry on his work with the boyos."

"Are you certain?" Mary Catherine said. "He was always a great one for family. Wouldn't he want you to be the protector of your sisters?"

Patrick stood mute before her, betraying only a brief look of defiance in answer to her question.

"He'd not want your dyin', Patrick," said his mother.

He led her to the hearth and there they sat together, her hands in his.

"Before you leave, I'll give you my decision," said Patrick. "Don't press me, Mother."

The phrase "before you leave" echoed in her mind. She'd come to the end of her argument. To say more would anger him Mary Catherine knew, so she held her tongue.

She yearned to put her arms about him and hold him. Leave him be she must, no matter how hard. With a sigh and heavy footed she crossed to the stacked dishes on the dry sink. Placing some plates in the dishpan, Mary Catherine turned and crossed to the wood stove to fetch the water Catherine had left heating there. With her back to him Patrick had softly deserted the house, leaving an emptiness in her.

When her daughters returned, Mary Catherine hid from

them the tears slipping into the dishwater as she grieved her anticipated loss of Patrick.

The following Sunday she and Martin met with the pastor to arrange their wedding. They would be married in the new church, St. Joseph's, in the spring.

With the closing of the mines for the winter, peace settled on the patch. Patrick spent more time at home, which pleased her, and helped his sisters with the marketing of her bread stuffs. Several evenings Martin stopped by to visit. Sitting with him before the warm hearth fire, Mary Catherine dwelt on what the coming years might bring.

The wedding day had been set for a week before Easter on a Saturday. On Friday evening before the wedding Patrick disappeared. A band of fear tightened its hold on Mary Catherine's heart. News of murder and mayhem in the coal fields had filtered through to Locust Gap and had involved some of the local lads. A certain Patrick Hester's name had been whispered about. So-called accidents happened with startling regularity in their patch, worrying Mary Catherine about the seduction of her son by such men. She understood that they were just trying to better their lives, such as they were. But Mary Catherine wanted Patrick to come away with her and be freed from the risk posed by his dangerous friends.

    Her misgivings brought such turmoil to her mind that she slept fitfully the night before her wedding. Come morning they would be married, and they would leave the patch the Monday after Easter. It had all been arranged. Between tossing and turning, Mary Catherine prayed most fervently, and, getting up several times, she knelt on the floor, hoping the hardness of the wood would add value to her pleas. Tears would not come to relieve her, for the forebodings of the night would not suffer such trivialities.

BRIDGET

Patrick did not return during the night, and in the morning panic raged within her. Mary Catherine presented a calm exterior for her daughters, though she could feel her face stretched taut with the strain of it. Dressing herself for her wedding, she tried to clothe herself in the festivity of the occasion both in mind and body. Mary Catherine counted the hours that passed till it came time for her to go to join Martin at St. Joseph's Church. Still no Patrick appeared. She couldn't keep Martin waiting any longer. Mary Catherine's daughters urged her to leave for the church.

The pungent scent of new wood and lacquer wafted over the wedding party as they formed a half circle before the altar. Joseph and John, Esther's two sons, stood alongside Martin on St. Joseph's side of the altar, and Mary Catherine's daughters took their places beside her on the Blessed Mother's side. Wearing a new blue dress, Mary Catherine carried a small bouquet of blue and white violets, and a crown of the same blooms dressed her hair, picked for her that very morning by her eldest daughter.

Turning to Catherine now to hand her the bouquet, Mary Catherine caught a movement in the back of the church. Peering into the shadows, she spied Patrick just slipping into a pew. Overcome with relief tears sprang to her eyes, which Mary Catherine hurriedly blinked away. Then turning to Martin, she gave him her trembling hand.

After the ceremony Mary Catherine searched among the faces of her friends for that special one she had glimpsed but briefly before the ceremony. She discovered Patrick and Martin shaking hands, a forced cordiality in both expressions. Although she vowed nothing would mar the gaiety of the day, nagging doubts ate away at her pleasure.

"What did Patrick have to say for himself?" said Mary Catherine, putting the question to her husband of only a few hours as they lay in their wedding bed that night.

"If you mean did he say if he would go or stay, he didn't say."

"What'll I do, Martin?"

"We'll leave on Monday as planned," said Martin.

"Without Patrick?" Mary Catherine asked.

"If need be, yes," said Martin. "He's a man by men's reckoning. He'll go or stay as he wishes."

There was peace in acceptance, she knew. She had fought long enough. She could battle her son no more. Mary Catherine slept wrapped in Martin's close embrace.

BRIDGET

CHAPTER XXXVI

Their belongings had been packed for several days. The oak table had been knocked down to carry, and Mary Catherine's dishes bundled in pine boxes The beds would be left behind, for Martin had promised to build new ones.

Mary Catherine gazed round the house she had known for more than fifteen years, mourning the loss of the life lived in it. Much of the woman she had become now bound up in its walls. Would they whisper of her to the newcomers? Looking round

BRIDGET   Johnson

again her vision unclouded by emotion, Mary Catherine saw it anew. A ramshackle affair of rough, furred floors bereft of its appurtenances it no longer held claim on her. With great care Mary Catherine closed the door behind her as she would on a parlor of grief.

Outside Martin stood waiting, and together they walked for the last time along the dusty patch road.

The smiling faces of her daughters' were the first she noticed amongst the crowd of well-wishers at the railroad siding. The girls' excitement over this adventure, although plain to see from the first, had surprised Mary Catherine. Thinking back on her own youth, she recalled the joy tinged with grieving with which she had abandoned her home to come to this new land. Mary Catherine smiled to herself over the comforting thought that her daughters in spite of their diverse temperaments held within them the self same boldness as herself.

"Mary Catherine," said Martin, "I'm going to check to make sure our things got on the train."

"Yes, Martin," Mary Catherine said. "And would you inquire after Patrick while you're about it?"

Martin, shaking his head, strode off in the direction of the smoke stack, puffing small, charred clouds a short distance away.

Spying Esther, Mary Catherine made her way to her friend's side.

"Are you and your sons ready for the journey?" said Mary Catherine.

"They're settling our goods on-board now," said Esther, chuckling. "They actually got up before dawn without urging. A first for them."

Annie with her son on her hip hailed them as she clumsily dog-trotted toward them.

"I've nothin' to give either of you for the trip," she said.

BRIDGET

"Jack's been out of work more days than not."

"Don't we all know that," said Esther.

"Annie, the bit of lace you gave me for my weddin' dress I'll cherish all my life long, don't you know," said Mary Catherine.

Gathering mother and son into her embrace, she kissed Annie on the cheek. All three women looked down the track to see if the train had started to move in their direction as yet. Continuing to chat with her friends, Mary Catherine sent furtive glances over their shoulders, still searching for that one elusive face.

Mary Catherine spotted Martin making his way toward them. His eyes met hers. A frown shifting his eyebrows indicated that he had not seen Patrick. Sighing with a regret that came from deep within her, Mary Catherine scrutinized each face in the crowd, sending pleas to heaven to make this errant son appear before her. But Patrick did not come.

"Fiona, where are your sisters?" said Mary Catherine.

BRIDGET   Johnson

"Just over there, Mama," Fiona said, pointing to a small gaggle of girls a few yards away.

"Tell them to come," said her mother. "They should say their goodbyes. We'll be boardin' the train soon now."

Prophetically a blast of steam accompanied by the steel monster's cry followed hard upon her words. Her daughters rushed up to her, their eyes wide with anticipation.

The little group watched as the shiny, black engine drew the long train of cars by the siding where they waited. The commotion of boarding busied them, and soon Martin had them all seated with Mary Catherine next to the window keeping vigil.

"Mary Catherine," said Esther, speaking to her from her seat across the narrow aisle. "You won't make him come, by wishing it so."

"I know," said Mary Catherine, turning to Esther. "But I can't help hopin'."

BRIDGET   Johnson

Once more Mary Catherine hunted through their neighbors' forest of waving hands outside the car's window, while her fingers picked anxiously at her calico skirt. Then with a jerk the train lurched forward, the clangor of metal on metal assaulting her ears as each car pulled taut. A lone tear traced aside her nose as she stared out the window, not really seeing the patch slipping by. Touching her cheek, Mary Catherine wiped away the drop, averting her face from the other passengers.

A hand touched her shoulder.

"I waved as I passed your window. But you didn't see me."

Patrick!

She had only taken her eyes from the scene outside for a moment. How could she have missed him?

"I see you now," Mary Catherine said, gazing up at him.

Sure'n my heart is full with the sight of you, Mary Catherine exulted, hoping her look conveyed her meaning.

BRIDGET

CHAPTER XXXVII

"Mama, a bunch of children are on this train," said Rose.

"I'm sure, Rose," Mary Catherine said, preoccupied with finding a comfortable position in which to endure the ride.

"But, Mama, there's a whole lot of them," said Rose. "It doesn't look like any family I've ever seen."

"You'll be seein' all kinds of strange things before this trip is over," said Mary Catherine.

After so many years in Locust Gap Mary Catherine had

BRIDGET   Johnson

almost forgotten the discomforts of travel. One improvement had been gained though. The trains no longer seemed to jump along. A steady clacking as cars passed over rails created an hypnotic rhythm, quieting the adults and sending infants off to sleep. Children played in the isles while the train rolled along.

When they stopped for the dinner hour, most of the passengers rushed to a village inn nearby. Martin led Mary Catherine and her children to a table in the corner for their meal. A luxury she hadn't been able to afford in her youth. Around another table a group of young children of varying ages gathered.

"See, Mama, there's the children I told you about," said Rose.

"So they are," Mary Catherine said. "Martin, do you know whose children they be?"

"I've heard they're orphans from the city," said Martin. "Some're orphans from the war, others from families too poor to keep their young'uns."

The children were only given bread and broth Mary Catherine noticed, whilst the waiters brought beef stew to the table at which her family sat. At least she believed the mess of potatoes and vegetables accompanied by large chunks of meat, swimming in oily brown gravy, to be stew.

"How long do they expect those children to live on that?" said Mary Catherine.

"Not long," said Martin.

She stared at her husband in dismay.

"It's not what you think," he said. "They're taking them out of the city to farms west of here."

"To be slave labor?" she said.

"That's not the idea," said Martin. "They hope to find good families for the homeless waifs."

The notion of transplanting children sat uneasy on Mary

BRIDGET   Johnson

Catherine. They're not potatoes after all to be plucked up and set down at will.

Back on board the train Mary Catherine noticed Patrick scratching his head. Fingering through his dark curls, she discovered a louse. She pinched it dead between her fingers, then threw it on the wooden floor to crush it under the heal of her shoe. Looking around, she marked others doing the same. Parents busied themselves, picking the vermin from their children and each other. Another consequence of overcrowding. Mary Catherine supposed she should be grateful they weren't dying of the ship's fever.

This worry had hardly left her mind, when the train, whistles screaming and brakes screeching, rounded a hill. The carriage shook hard enough to be rid of them entirely, halting on a bit of track that clung to the side of a low mountain. The sudden stop stirred alarm in Mary Catherine. Time passed and the train's crew made no effort to start up again. Some of the passengers ventured to climb down from their cars to discover the cause of their delay. Patrick held her hand as he with Martin on her other side helped her scramble down from their car. Following their fellow travelers, Mary Catherine had just reached the engine, when Martin, who had gone ahead, strode toward her.

"The bridge isn't safe to cross," he said.

"Not safe to cross?" said Mary Catherine. "How long'll we be here?"

"They could back the train to the last siding," said Martin, "but they decided to fix the bridge instead. They'll have us on our way by nightfall, they say."

"I suppose it could be worse," she said. "It'll just mean waitin'."

"You could have the children walk about and stretch their legs a bit," Martin said. "I'll be waiting for you down the track."

BRIDGET   Johnson

"And just where might you be goin'?" Mary Catherine demanded.

"Someone has to walk to the next station and warn them to put the next train through onto the siding," said Martin. "I volunteered."

"I thought you said your war experiences taught you not to do that."

Shuffling from foot to foot, Martin's lips curved in a sheepish grin.

"It's not the same, Mary Kate, and you know it."

Here they were, stranded, and she was quibbling about what she knew he must do. Since when had she become so dependent on any man? Going to Martin, Mary Catherine took his hand in hers and kissed him on the cheek.

"Go if you must," she said.

Stepping carefully from tie to tie across the bridge, Martin stopped midway to give her that broad smile of his, then disappeared around the bend on the other side of the crevasse.

"Very well, girls, have a walk-around, and, Patrick, mind you don't wander too far," said Mary Catherine, "or you'll get left behind."

During their forced rest, Mary Catherine and Esther found a pleasant spot on a hillside overlooking the Susquehanna River, whose waters sparkled through the trees far below the broken trestle. All in all a pleasant stop Mary Catherine mused as she and Esther settled down in the tall grass to enjoy the view.

The men had restored the trestle by twilight, and travel resumed its monotonous routine of stop and go for fuel and water. With Martin once again by her side Mary Catherine's fears only rose on the rare occasion, when she might be gazing out the window and find herself staring into a rocky abyss.

About dinnertime one day Mary Catherine spied blackened

clouds rising above the distant horizon. Could it be a fire? Her apprehension mounted as they drew nearer the imagined conflagration.

"It's Pittsburgh, Mary Kate," Martin said, smiling broadly.

"What causes the fumin'?" said Mary Catherine.

"The furnaces," Martin said. "That's where some of the coal is shipped that we mined. To make steel."

"It is, is it?" said Mary Catherine. "How can people breathe air so choked with soot?"

"I don't know," Martin said. "But you won't have to worry about that where we're going."

They changed trains in the sprawling rail yard. The largest she'd seen since traveling through New Jersey many years before. Mary Catherine held a corner of her shawl over her nose and mouth, protecting herself from the grit that threatened to choke her. Even in the dirty streets of Liverpool and New York she'd not smelled anything so vile. They'd no sooner settled themselves in the rail-car, then they were told they'd be crossing another river in a matter of hours. After the rush for the crowded ferry they stood elbow to elbow on-board, waiting to dock on the far shore of the Ohio River. Once on board the next train they waited and waited. No one dared get off for fear of being left behind.

"Martin, we have no food left," Mary Catherine said. "When might we be able to get more?"

"I'm not sure," said Martin. "I'll try to arrange for something at the next town. Hopefully they'll stop for supper."

The train seemed to Mary Catherine to be some kind of faceless monster that swallowed up humans to spit them out on a whim and gobble up more, stopping only where and when it pleased. She knew it to be but a fancy, but what else was there to do but fret?

Once started the train didn't halt till long after dark.

BRIDGET   Johnson

Everyone rushed the exits. After disembarking Mary Catherine hesitated. Her eyes becoming accustomed to the pitch, black night, all she could discern were the elongated legs of a water tower. Not a single light betrayed the existence of any establishment that could provide victuals.

Startled, she yelped at the cool touch on her arm.

"I'm sorry, Mary Catherine. I'm afraid there'll be nothing to eat this night," said Martin. "Seems the engineer passed up the only town of a size to carry provisions for so many. He's trying to make up time, he says."

"It won't be the first time I've gone hungry," Mary Catherine said. "But the children should have something."

"The train'll have to stop in the morning," said Martin. "They're setting down some of the orphans then."

Just at daybreak the train halted at a station, the sun glowing ruddy on the horizon as the orphan children lined up on the platform. Descending from the car, Mary Catherine watched, puzzling over how they would be chosen.

"Mary Kate, let's go to the dining hall," said Martin. "There's not much time."

"All right," she said. "I just wondered what would be happenin' to the mites."

"They'll be just fine. Come now."

After gulping down a plateful of greasy fried potatoes and cold beans, they rushed back to the train. The orphans still stood on the platform.

"The children have had nothin' to eat, Martin," said Mary Catherine. "It's a sin and a shame to let them go starvin'."

"As soon as they're chosen, someone'll feed them," Martin said.

"What about the ones that aren't chosen?"

"It's not up to us, Mary Kate."

BRIDGET   Johnson

"Who then, Martin?"

"We have to get on board," he said.

Her audacious spirit heaved in rebellion.

"They have to have something, Martin," Mary Catherine said, resolution growing in her nurturing heart. "I've a bit of money. I'm goin' to get them some bread at least."

Mary Catherine turned and sprinted the short distance to the dining hall. Once inside she negotiated a platter of golden baked rolls, scooped them up, wrapped them in newsprint, and, placing the bundle in her shawl, hurried with her precious package back to the depot. The children gathered around her, each clamoring for their share. Looking over her shoulder as she boarded the train, Mary Catherine glimpsed the children chewing in earnest with smiles on their faces. A warm feeling crowded the pit of her stomach.

The train didn't pull away till choices had been made by

the community's farmers and townsfolk. Those children not chosen climbed back into the cars, and they were off to repeat this performance at several more stations along their route. After dinner in Columbus the train raced through the night. They slept sitting up on hard, wooden seats with only each other to lean on. Several nights of this had caused a pain in her back that brought intermittent sleep at best to Mary Catherine. Just before dawn she noticed they were pulling off on a siding and nudged Martin awake.

"Martin, I'm goin' to get off for a minute," Mary Catherine said. "I've got to give my back a rest."

He grunted acknowledgment, then leaned against the coach wall and readily fell asleep.

Upon alighting, she saw that other passengers had done the same. Mary Catherine had just started forward along the train, when she felt an arm slip through hers.

BRIDGET Johnson

"Esther, you near took a year off my life comin' up behind me like that."

"Where are you going?" said Esther.

"Just takin' a turn," Mary Catherine said.

"A body gets stiff all right, sitting so long," said Esther.

Noticing a cluster of passengers babbling excitedly, the two friends, curious as to the cause, approached them to inquire.

"What's happened?" asked Esther.

"Seems we'll be here awhile," said one of the men. "There's been a wreck about a mile up the track."

"Too much rushing," said another. "Not enough track. They hit head-on."

"Was anyone hurt?" asked Mary Catherine.

"Some dead, I expect. It's that hard they hit."

Mary Catherine glanced at Esther, who nodded in turn.

They searched out the engineer and announced their

intention of going up the track to offer their assistance. He couldn't go with them, he explained. His duty was to stay with his engine. He warned them to return before the track was cleared.

Mary Catherine and Esther boarded the train again, gathering cloth and sewing needles, and other paraphernalia they might need to nurse the injured.

"Martin, there's been an accident up the track," Mary Catherine said, rousing her husband. "Esther and me are goin' to help."

"I'll come along."

"It's not necessary. Esther's boys and Patrick are comin'. It's nurses they'll be needin'."

"I'll see to the girls then," he said.

"We'll be back quick enough," she said, kissing him on the cheek.

She gathered her skirt and bundle in one hand and swung

BRIDGET   Johnson

down from the train.

    Walking the track in the ashen predawn hours, the two women, escorted by Esther's sons and Patrick, hurried their steps, for gathering clouds presaged stormy weather on the horizon. Wet splotches spattered them just as they caught sight of an engine toppled into a ravine alongside the track. This engine's cow-catcher pointed toward another engine also tumbled into the ditch. Many people ran about, some helping, others appearing to have lost their wits. Picking their way through the rain, wind, and throng, the two women heard the crying of children, women, and men amidst the moaning and screams of agony that came from the mangled iron.

    "Esther, did you happen to bring a bucket?"

    "One of my boys did."

    "Good. I think I heard a stream down there somewhere," Mary Catherine said. "One of the boys should go for water."

"I'll get it," said Esther. "The boys'll be busy pulling bodies out of the wreck."

A streak of lightning revealed the scene. A giant had been at play and had carelessly strewn the cars about in a fit of pique. Smoke now rose from some of the cars, fire fueled by the lanterns that had lit the carriages. Groping amongst the bodies laid prone upon the ground, Mary Catherine found them already cold to the touch. She looked up to see a conductor coming toward her, his cap missing from his head and blood running down his face.

"Hey there, what're you doing there?"

"Some of us have come to help," said Mary Catherine. "Our train is stopped up the track there."

"If you want to help, follow me."

Esther, lugging the water bucket, fell into step, and the two women obediently followed the trainman. John, Joseph, and Patrick joined the other men and helped to locate the living and

BRIDGET   Johnson

brought them to where the women could minister to them. Some with cuts and gashes Esther stitched back together, having learned how to sew torn flesh during the war. Mary Catherine washed blood and dirt from wounds and set broken bones. Bloodied rain nourished the ground beneath her feet. By midday they had done all that they could and, thoroughly soaked, Esther and Mary Catherine returned to their train to dry themselves and rest. Their sons stayed a while longer to sort out the dead. The bodies would either be claimed by family or buried alongside the track.

    Once the railroad was cleared and everyone had boarded, their train sped off, racing to make up time wasted in the wait. Mary Catherine hoped as the train accelerated that they'd not meet with a similar fate. Praying more than one prayer for her friends and family, she added another for the poor souls who had met their end that day.

    Later when she woke Mary Catherine noticed smoke once

again on the horizon. Could it be another city with puffing smokestacks? The clouds of smoke appeared to hover just over the treetops. Looking round the car, Mary Catherine wondered if the sight had alarmed anyone else. Calm met her gaze.

The door at the end of the car opened, and Martin strode toward her.

"Mary Catherine, don't be frightened," he said, "but the woods up ahead are on fire."

"Aren't we goin' to stop?" said Mary Catherine.

"No, we're not," Martin said. "The engineer says stopping won't help. The wind's in the wrong direction. He's going to run it."

"Mary, Mother of God, save us," Mary Catherine said, looking fearfully out the window. "What'll become of us?"

Flames now licked up through the smoke. Just as she stared at the fire mesmerized, a ball of fire shot up into the sky shocking her loose from her fascination. Other passengers, becoming aware of their plight, shrieked with terror. A few men jumped from the speeding train to save themselves. The rest, including Mary Catherine and her family, huddled together in the aisle away from the car's wooden walls. Children cried out, and mothers cooed in an effort to calm them.

"Put something over your mouth and nose!" Martin shouted above the roar of the conflagration. "And cover your heads!"

"Do as Martin says," said Mary Catherine. "Use your skirts, my girls."

Smoky haze invaded the car, choking everyone, stinging Mary Catherine's eyes, making it impossible for her to see anything, even human forms. Glass shattered and she watched as the flames reach into the car, consuming all before it till it was glutted and reaching for more. Putting her head down, Mary Catherine felt the heat caress her back, and she swept her hand over her head to keep her hair from burning. The living flame licked her arm, blistering it. She bit her lip, for she dared not cry out for fear of endangering anyone coming to her aid.

The occasional glimpse, whenever Mary Catherine dared to raise her head, afforded her a view of walls of red-hot flame on both sides of the car as the train rushed through burning hell. When would it end? Would they live?

Brakes wailed as the train bucked against the stoppage.

"Come, children," shouted Mary Catherine, "get out."

Leading the way, Mary Catherine rushed forward with her skirt over her head, walls burning around her. With no time for modesty her mind focused on surviving the firestorm. Mary Catherine jumped from the step, rolling on the ground.

Once away from the railroad and the burning car she stood, brushed her skirt down, and searched about for her family and friends. Spying her eldest daughter, Mary Catherine pressed

BRIDGET Johnson

forward through the tall, prairie grass to Catherine.

"Catherine Marie, where are your sisters?" Mary Catherine said. "Have you seen them?"

"Here, Mama, right behind me."

Catherine pushed her sisters before her for their mother's inspection. Overcome with relief to see them unharmed Mary Catherine threw her arms about them all, tears of relief moistening her cheeks.

After releasing them, she stepped back and gazed at their soot, blackened faces, a giggle bubbling up her throat. Her lips parted and the laugh burst forth.

"You look like you've spent a week in the mines," said Mary Catherine.

Her girls glanced at each other then pointed their fingers at her.

"You too, Mama," said Catherine.

They giggled, then laughed heartily, and fell on the ground convulsing hysterically.

"And just what's so funny about almost being burned alive, I'd like to know."

Esther stomped towards them her blonde braids all askew, sticking up in all directions with the ends scorched black. Sitting up, Mary Catherine watched her friend advance on them.

"Esther, if only you could see yourself."

Mary Catherine could stand it no longer. Hugging her sides, she gave in to the perverseness of the moment. Esther, plunking herself down beside her, laughed loudest of all.

Spent, they lay in the grass.

"When you women have done with your fun, we'll be moving along," Martin said, approaching the women as they rose to shake out and smooth their skirts.

"Is the train able to travel, Martin?" Mary Catherine asked.

BRIDGET	Johnson

"Our car and some others burned. But we'll pack ourselves in somewhere."

"Are the boys all right?" asked Esther.

"Your sons and Patrick are fine," said Martin. "We've been putting out the fire on the train."

Slowly the passengers boarded the cars, which still smelled of charred wood. Everyone did their best to make room for each other even though more cramped for space. Tearing a small piece from the bottom of her shift, Mary Catherine wiped the soot from her daughters' faces and once more settled in to suffer the tiresome, endless running of the tracks.

Raining steadily for several days thereafter, Mary Catherine presumed there would be no more fires to contend with. The relief this brought to her mind allowed her to rest in spite of backache and noise. Waking with an urgent need to use the convenience, Mary Catherine went behind the curtain that covered a scant box of a place, containing a slop bucket. After relieving herself, she emerged to find that the train had halted, a fact she had already guessed from the jerky, slowing motion.

Once back in her seat Mary Catherine touched Martin's shoulder.

"Martin, why are we stopped this time?" she whispered.

"Are we?" he said, rubbing the sleep from his eyes and looking about. "So we are."

"But, why?" said Mary Catherine. "I've looked. There's nothin' out there."

The steady staccato of rain on the roof and water streaming down the car's windows proved that heaven's largess of moisture had not yet come to an end. Glancing about the car, Mary Catherine noted that their whispering had not disturbed anyone. Together they made their way to the back of the car in the dim light of a single lamp, and a wall of darkness greeted them on the steps

BRIDGET   Johnson

as they felt their way down from the car to the ground.

Glancing first up the track then down Mary Catherine spied a lantern's dim glow near the engine.

"Wait here, Mary Kate," said Martin. "I'll see what's happening."

Watching Martin make his way along the train, rain now dripped from her nose and hair soaking her bodice.

"Might as well get back aboard," Martin said upon his return. "No use our standing here. It's going to be a long wait."

Martin took her by the elbow, ushering her up the steps again into the car.

Once back inside she noticed some of the passengers stirring.

"Why aren't we moving?" one passenger asked, tugging at her skirt.

Pulling her dress free, she sat down on a bench with Martin

sitting down beside her.

"Now Martin, what is it?" said Mary Catherine.

"All this rain. A river up ahead has washed out the railroad bridge."

"What'll we do? Surely we can't wait here till they build a new one."

"I guess people have," Martin said just above a whisper. "But they haven't made a decision yet. One of the men has taken shank's mare to the nearest station to ask what to do."

"Meanwhile we're expected to just sit and wait till they make up their minds, are we?" Mary Catherine said, her voice rising.

"Mary Kate, keep your voice down. No good'll come from alarming the rest."

"You're right," she said. "But I'm beginnin' to think we're never goin' to get to the end of it."

BRIDGET

"We most certainly will get to the end of it, as you say," Martin said, putting his arm around her and drawing her close. "You're a strong woman and you'll make it just fine."

BRIDGET

CHAPTER XXXVIII

In the end the railway company sent wagons to carry them over rutted roads to another station further north. There they were told a train would take them to Chicago in the morning. Getting down from the wagon with Martin's assistance, Mary Catherine rubbed the soreness from her buttocks in a surreptitious fashion, hoping no one would notice. She glanced about and discovered fare set upon tables for them in a sunny field near the station.

"Catherine, Fiona, Rose," called Mary Catherine. "One of

BRIDGET   Johnson

you go tell your brother, there's food to be had just there."

"He already knows, Mama," said Rose, beaming at Mary Catherine. "His nose told him so," she added, seeming quite pleased with her cleverness.

Not expecting much from a repast served up in the wilderness, Mary Catherine approached the table with caution. Pungent smells of roast venison greeted her, and pheasant, lake trout, and stewed wild birds covered the board. Roasted potatoes rested well on her tongue, and she delighted in the breads almost as crusted and soft centered as her own. Plain women, smiling as they worked, served them coffee, tea, and spring water to wash down the victuals. Not knowing who to thank for such a generous banquet Mary Catherine outdid herself by thanking everyone within reach.

"Martin, who's to pay for such a wonderful meal?"

"No one, Mary Kate," Martin said. "The town folk heard

about the disaster and the long dirty ride we had, and they just decided to show us a kindness."

"I've not had such goodness from strangers since I came to this country."

"Where we're going I think we'll find many such as these generous souls," he said. "People depend on each other on the land."

The village boasted no hotel, boarding house, tavern, or inn, affording only a train depot with a roofed platform for shelter. The women and children found comfort that night on the depot floor, while the men slept outside on the wooden platform.

Coffee redolent on the morning air woke Mary Catherine just before dawn. A huge cauldron of mush bubbled over an open fire, and fresh bread along with the leavings of the feast from the evening before rounded out the menu. A babble of gratitude rose from the group seated around the tables for the unexpected bounty provided by the village and farm families, who appeared embarrassed by the effusion of such appreciation.

Just as the glow on the horizon apprised everyone of daybreak, a familiar blast heralded the approaching train. A tight fit she found the train car to be when Mary Catherine boarded. Looking around her, she discovered there to be little room even for standing and puzzled about where Esther and her sons had fitted themselves in.

"Catherine, where's Patrick?" said Mary Catherine.

"He's chummin' in the next car, Mama."

"Sleepin' with a stranger?" said Mary Catherine. "No guessin' what he might catch from doin' that."

Returning from having a pipe outside on the platform, Martin stood over her.

"What's causin' such crowdin', Martin?" said Mary Catherine.

"We're headed for Chicago, Mary Kate. I hear it's quite the city."

"You mean everybody on this train is goin' there?"

"No, but most are," Martin said. "Some like us will be changing trains there."

"Well, I hope there'll be more sittin' room then," said Mary Catherine.

"Once we're away from the city there should be," Martin said.

They endured the interminable start and stop of taking on wood and water and rushing to obtain the odd bit to eat. Mary Catherine, wearying of the journey that took so long to finish, wondered when they would rest. Age had never bothered her much before. This constant moving consumed her. Baking her breads every morning in the gap had not taxed her so. She began to wish it all would end. The beauty of the land, and it was

BRIDGET   Johnson

considerable she had to admit, did not entice her as once it had. Gazing listlessly out the window, Mary Catherine focused on nothing at all. She said naught to Martin, for she had no wish to dishearten him, feeling it to be her burden alone and none of his account.

Dozing lightly, her nostrils flared as she became aware of a change in the air. The smell churned her stomach as the train drew closer to something quite disagreeable. Sitting up ramrod straight, Mary Catherine peered out the window, scrutinizing the green and inviting countryside as they past. Suspecting the source of the foul sour air, Mary Catherine held her nose against the sickening odor.

"Mama, what is it?" said Fiona.

"I'm not sure, Fiona," Mary Catherine said. "But it smells like pigs to me."

Martin had been sitting on the floor napping with his back against the car wall. Chuckling could be heard coming from him, though his chin still rested on his chest.

"Is it laughin' you are, Martin Kass?" said Mary Catherine.

Lifting his head, he guffawed with gusto.

"And pray, what is the joke?" she asked.

"It's not funny, I guess," Martin said, his sniggering choked off as he reined in his fun. "It's the stockyards. Welcome to Chicago."

"You mean a city smells like that?" said Mary Catherine.

"Not all the city, just the train yards," he said. "The place has become a center for the meat trade on the hoof, I've heard tell."

"I guess we can put up with it," said Mary Catherine. "Now that I think back on it, New York smelled none too sweet either. Human stock that we were."

In the sultry heat of the day the passengers detrained with the stench of livestock droppings, urine, and rot assaulting their sensitivities to such a pitch that several way-farers retched on descent. Herding her family ahead of her, Mary Catherine took great care where she planted each foot to avoid stepping into the dung so recently disgorged from animal bowels.

"How long will we be here, Martin?" said Mary Catherine. "Will we have a chance to find something edible?"

"I'll go and ask the ticket master," Martin said, "and see if there's any food to be had."

They had entered the depot, a huge barn of a place. Many people milled about, and a chuckle threatened to escape Mary Catherine's lips as she gazed at the throng. And all the cattle may not be out in the stockyards, she mused. For just look at us.

"Mama, are we goin' to eat?" said Rose.

"Martin's lookin' into that, Rose," Mary Catherine said. "Be patient."

"But, Mama, are we goin' to another country?" said Fiona.

BRIDGET

"It's takin' that long."

"And how would you be knowin' anything about that, my girl?"

Boarding the train took longer than Mary Catherine had reckoned. The changing of cars, loading and unloading, and hitching them together again made one wonder. Meanwhile Martin found bread and a little milk to guard against hunger. Twilight came upon them. Then the call came.

"All aboard."

They rushed. They sat. They waited. Finally, movement. Mary Catherine hadalmost given up hope they'd get started that day. The rhythm would have put her to sleep, but for the stink. She'd have to inhale a great deal of a fresh air to cleanse her nostrils of the fair city of Chicago. Sitting in the dark, Mary Catherine recalled how far she'd come from home. I've put an ocean between me and thee, she reflected. They were right to have

BRIDGET								Johnson

a wake, for I'll truly never see Ireland again. And as she slept the dreams came. The visions of father, mother, son, brother, babes, and the ould country, quieted in her now.

    Balmy air wakened her as light filtered through the smoke befouled windows. Martin had managed to open the one nearest her, and the odor of dew laden grass and wild flowers drove away the memory of the previous day and its unpleasantness. Sitting up, Mary Catherine straightened and smoothed her dress over her lap.

    Then a sound came to her that she didn't recognize, a screeching whining thing. And the train came to a slipping, sliding, careening halt. Mary Catherine stuck her head out the window and searched in both directions, spying neither town nor fueling station.

    "Now what?" Mary Catherine said, turning to her husband.

    Martin shrugged his shoulders in answer.

    "And to think I had hopes," said Mary Catherine. "Would

it be askin' too much, Martin, if you'd go and inquire."

"Not a'tall wife," Martin replied.

Kissing her on the forehead as if pacifying a spoiled child, he left her. Mary Catherine rose and with her hands on her hips watched him go.

"Girls, you stay on the train," Mary Catherine said, turning to her daughters. "I'm gettin' down to see for myself."

As she backed off the lowest step Mary Catherine turned to find Patrick walking along the track toward her.

"Do you know what it's about, Patrick?"

"It's nothin', Mother," said Patrick. "Grasshoppers, that's all."

"How could insects stop a train?"

"The locusts grease the track," said Patrick. "The wheels crush'em."

"You needn't go any further," she said, waving off the

BRIDGET

illustration.

Her son having helped her back up the steps, Mary Catherine informed her daughters of the reason for the delay.

"Mary Kate, they're sanding the tracks now," said Martin, upon entering the car. "We'll soon be on our way. Nothing but a trifling, considering."

A sigh of relief escaped her nonetheless. Mary Catherine could do without further excitement, the adventure beginning to wear thin on her. The prairie soon gave way to hills and streams. The very scene Mary Catherine had envisioned in Pennsylvania, only to be let down. The ennui of her travels left her. Truly this must be God's own land. Enlivened by the sight of it the young lass she once had been quickened again within her. The green of the land, the blue of the sky welcomed her home.

BRIDGET

CHAPTER XXXIX

"We'll be passing by the home of the General," said Martin.

"And what general might that be?"

"General Grant, of course, Mary Kate."

"Well, he's the president now, is he not," Mary Catherine said. "What town is it we're passin'?"

"Galena," said Martin. "And we'll be at the river soon after."

BRIDGET

"Will a riverboat be takin' us where we're goin'?"

"Not quite. We'll get on a ferry, which'll take us for a bit. Then we'll board a paddle wheeler to go up river."

The smaller vessel reminded her of her first steamboat ride many years before, overcrowded and with no amenities to speak of. That evening they docked on the great river, the Mississippi.

In the crush of the railroad cars Mary Catherine had frequently lost sight of Esther and her sons. On the dock the following morning she searched the crowded wharf for the familiar face of her friend. Spying Esther approaching from lands end, Mary Catherine waved to her.

"Will you be goin' up river with us, Esther?"

"Yes, we will," said Esther. "My sons have heard the land up river is rich for farming."

They went aboard the riverboat within the hour, but unlike trains the freight had been loaded the night before. Horns blasted their departure and the boat glided away from the shore into mid-river. The smoothness of the ride pleasantly surprised Mary Catherine, since she had experienced all manner of discomfort in her travels. Albeit the current prevented any speed she rather enjoyed the slow slide along the muddy waterway.

Esther and Mary Catherine strolled the deck engaged in speculation about what lay beyond the river.

"What are your hopes, Esther?" Mary Catherine asked her friend.

"A small farm. Wives for my sons. Grandchildren to hold upon my knee," said Esther. "And a rocking chair on the porch for my old age."

"I've been disappointed in the places I've been since comin' to this country," Mary Catherine said. "I think I'll not be weavin' fancies about this one."

"That's probably best. Only God knows what we'll find."

BRIDGET   Johnson

They strolled on arm in arm in the last rays of the setting sun.

Horns and whistles wailed, startling Mary Catherine awake. Thinking it had to be a disaster, she dressed hurriedly and left the cabin before Martin and the children. Outside on the deck in the predawn light she spied her son.

"Patrick, do you know what all the racket's about?" said Mary Catherine.

"It's a race, Mama."

"A race?" said Mary Catherine. "What in heaven's name for?"

"Seems another steamboat challenged our captain, and he means to oblige them."

Patrick's excitement provoked misgivings in her.

The lazy progress of the day before now gave way to the rushing of water past the bow. She much preferred the calmer pace than trees flying by on the river bank before her very eyes. Mary Catherine clasped her son's warm hand in her own cold one.

"Can the boat stand the punishment, Patrick?" she said.

"I should think so, Mother," Patrick replied, squeezing her hand and smiling down at her.

Her attention riveted on the black smoke belching from the smokestacks, while the deck of the paddle wheeler shuddered under her feet with the engine's striving. People gathered on both decks cheering the captains on, while Mary Catherine clucked her tongue at their recklessness. The channel narrowed, driving the boats closer, and the passengers hurled taunts at each other, while bets were made on the outcome.

On they sped.

"Mary Catherine, what are these crazy men doing?" Esther cried, hurrying toward her.

"I'm beginnin' to wonder, Esther. I don't think what

they're doin' can be safe."

Just then Mary Catherine heard what sounded like a cannon's roar. She and Esther stared at each other. Then taking up their skirts, they ran round the boat to the side facing deep river and saw black smoke and flames amidships on the other paddle wheeler. People climbed the rails of the crippled vessel, standing ready to jump into the swift current. Another explosion sent floor boards and scarlet flares shooting skyward. Bodies fell into the river followed by screams and pleas for help. In the glare of the burning vessel Mary Catherine watched them sink out of sight as the river sucked them down.

The crippled paddle wheeler, turned sideways by the current, floated haplessly, while the river tore at her. The captain of their own boat held her steady, slowing to pick up what survivors they could reach with pikes and ropes. Only a few men were pulled aboard. Women with their heavy skirts had sunk quickly, and the children had not the strength to fight the river.

Laying in her bunk that night, Mary Catherine couldn't erase the day's scene from her mind, and sleep eluded her.

"Martin, are you awake?" she whispered.

"Yes, Mary Kate."

"Why did they do it?" Mary Catherine said. "Why did the captains race when it could mean certain death?"

No answer came to her from the other side of the bed. Her words from many years before came back to her out of the dark. Men will do what men will do.

BRIDGET

CHAPTER XL

After several stops to load more cargo and passengers they reached St. Anthony Falls, where Martin procured a small wagon and a pair of horses. Come sundown they camped beside a small stream. Martin built a fire from wood gathered by Joseph, John, and Patrick, while Mary Catherine and Esther cooked a camp supper. They were to be neighbors, for at the land recorder's office the men had bargained for land near each other.

The next morning they passed through a small village.

BRIDGET

Rattling and jarring down a wagon road, Mary Catherine's bones complained with every jolt. They came to a fork in the road, where Esther and her sons turned south, and Martin drove toward the northwest. Riding uphill and down, they rounded a bend. Her husband, commanding his new team, urged them up a path almost hidden by bushes and trees crowding upon it. Emerging through a grove of pines, Martin halted the team after he drove them to the crown of a hill. He then handed Mary Catherine down from the wagon seat, leaving the children to look after themselves. Below the crest to the east lay a wide lake, rippling with a quick breeze that wound Mary Catherine's skirt about her legs. The green of the waving grass, the white and yellow blooms that peeked through the blades, the rustle of the leaves in the trees, and the rise and fall of the land held in them a dream of Erin.

"All of this is ours," said Martin, taking a step forward and sweeping his arm across the scene.

BRIDGET — Johnson

Could such riches of earth and sky belong to anyone? The wonder of it caught at her heart.

Moving to her husband's side, Mary Catherine asked, "Where would you be buildin' our home, Martin?"

"I thought here," he said, putting his arm around her waist. "Would you like that?"

"'Tis a grand place for a new beginnin'," said Mary Catherine, smiling up at him.

And miracle she knew in that moment that they would build a future here.

Gazing again at the panorama before her, the smell of the earth and growing things reminded her of what grew within. Should she tell him now? 'Twas as good a time as any.

"Martin, God has blessed us," Mary Catherine said. "We're goin' to have an addition to the family. Could we be after callin' him Sean, if 'tis a boy?"

BRIDGET

CHAPTER XLI

EPILOGUE

Locust Gap, Pennsylvania

April 10, 1879

Dear Mary Catherine,

It has been years since I last wrote you. You're maybe thinking I must have died. Well there were times when I almost longed for it.

BRIDGET   Johnson

Jack is home again. So I take pen in hand to tell you what has been happening. We are all well. And so you might ask why not write and say so?

I knew you had a new life without the sorrows of the old. Now that it is past I can speak of it.

You remember Jack was going to the meetings at the pub again before you left. About five years ago things got real bad here. Mine buildings were blown and railroad track was torn up, causing cars to jump the tracks. Men were thrown out of work by hateful bosses. There was a strike. A long one. Jack spent more and more time away from home. He sometimes traveled with other men to mining patches miles away. Many a time I held my breath till he came home.

One day about a year ago he didn't come back. He and another Locust Gap boyo, Patrick Hester by name, were arrested along with some other men. Something they said happened years

BRIDGET   Johnson

ago in a place called Centralia. It's been whispered that Patrick Hester was a "Molly Maquire". We think 'tis a lie. He belonged to the Ancient Order of Hibernians and to a union of sorts.

But no one believes he was a Molly. A man named Bannan, who publishes a paper hereabouts, always blamed the Irish for all the evil done around here. We think he invented the "Molly Maguires".

They kept Jack in jail for several weeks, but let him go because no one would stand witness against him. Would you believe the company owners had a traitorous spy going around pointing the finger at some of our men. And one of the boyos also informed on them.

Then the hangings began. It took a year for the trials to be over and two more for the hangings to be done. Some of us from the gap went to Patrick Hester's hanging. Jack said he would go, and I wasn't about to let him out of my sight. I hope never to see

BRIDGET   Johnson

anyone hung again. The sight is with me still. Patrick and the others had ropes put round their necks. Then at a signal the floor gave way, and we could see their feet kicking and twitching. After a few minutes they were quiet. There they hung till their faces started to turn dark purple and swelled up.

You and I have seen things in the ould country. But death was different there even with the starving. Hanging. Hanging is worse than shooting a fella.

But you're just as dead whether it be by starving or hanging. The bosses have it all their own way now. We dare not say anything.

Jack's been black-listed. So we'll be moving to another town looking for work. He knows nothing but mining and won't try for anything else. Our Sean is big and strong now and helps by picking up the odd job. He does well with his schooling. Our hopes are in him.

BRIDGET   Johnson

May Jesus, Mary, and Joseph bless you and all in your house.

Your dear friend,

Anne Marie Byrnes

Made in the USA
Lexington, KY
28 September 2017